NEVERGREEN

A Novel

by
Andrew Pessin

PRAISE FOR *NEVERGREEN*

"Sharp, funny, and ultimately scary, *Nevergreen* cuts right to the quick of campus cancel culture and the ideological excesses that generate it. It may officially be a satire but it may as well be a documentary, it's so close to home. That something so serious can also be so entertaining is impressive."
   —William Jacobson, Cornell University

"Welcome to Nevergreen, a small college in full descent into madness. Intelligent and witty, with crackling dialogue and keenly planted in the cultural firmament, *Nevergreen* engages from start to finish. More *Animal Farm* than *Animal House*. Be prepared to be offended and like it."
   —Scott Johnston, author of Amazon bestseller, *Campusland*

"One part *Lucky Jim* and three parts *One Flew Over the Cuckoo's Nest*, Andrew Pessin's terrific and terrifying novel may just be the great campus novel of our generation. Every page delivers a hearty laugh, and every laugh soon blooms into a painful stab of recognition, reminding us that we're all stuck on Nevergreen. As bloody, apocalyptic, dystopian fantasies go, this one is a pure delight."
   —Liel Leibovitz, editor at large, *Tablet Magazine*

"A biting satire of a college campus driven literally mad with political correctness. Funny, disturbing, and thought-provoking, *Nevergreen* will change the way you look at college life."
   —Michael Satlow, Brown University

"*Nevergreen* is so painful I wanted to stop; yet so funny I kept going. Pessin has written a delirious yet detailed roman à clé for almost any campus today. Parody imitates life as Kafka wanders through Wokeland. In its own outrageous way, a triumph of sanity."
   —**Richard Landes, Boston University**

"In a novel bristling with verbal wit, Andrew Pessin weaves a tale around the social justice warrior culture and where it might take the campus. This funny book is ideal for scholars to read as we begin withdrawing from our zoom boxes for the airport and for travel to in-person conferences."
   —**Donna Robinson Divine, Smith College**

"*Nevergreen* is a happily diabolical satire of a woker than woke campus that hyperbolically mirrors current academic reality. Pessin shoots barbs at the Right as well as the Left as he depicts a manic game of musical chairs among student groups jockeying for credibility by 'hating hate.' While we watch the whirligig of time bringing its revenges on the Virtue Patrols now auditioning for the role of Big Brother, we can divert ourselves with Pessin, a delightful and sardonic kibitzer."
   —**David Mikics, University of Houston**

"Think a brilliant case of David Lodge meets *1984*. You laugh until you realize just how close this is to reality. Pessin updates the academic novel to include cancel culture and virtue signaling. Strongly, strongly recommended."
   —**Peter Herman, San Diego State University**

"Mix academic parody with Kafka-esque paranoia and a mounting *Lord of the Flies* drumbeat, and you wind up trapped on a dystopian island college (and former mental asylum), Nevergreen."
   —**Larry Silver, University of Pennsylvania**

CONTENTS

PART I
Welcome To The Asylum   1

PART II
You Are In Great Danger Here   45

PART III
Something Is Rotten On This Campus   77

PART IV
Kill The Beast! Cut His Throat! Spill His Blood!   111

THE LAST WORD   200

PART I

WELCOME TO THE ASYLUM

1

HE SAW HER FROM ten rows away, as she was coming down the aisle. The heavy bubble-themed sweater, the warm smile cast indiscriminately at the other passengers as she bobbed along. He dropped his eyes, anxiously glanced at the empty seat next to him, braced himself for the inevitable. "Good morning, friend!" the woman exuberated as she slipped her carry-on overhead and her carrion into the seat beside him.

Oh, good one, he thought; remember to tell Debra.

But now what to do? It was a long flight. The opening salvo could transition into an hours-long interchange. He was sure she was a wonderful person but that didn't mean he should want to hear her story. He was sure he was himself not a bad person and he had no need to tell *his* story, he reminded himself. His fingers tightened on the book in his hand. This tome by Eco that Debra had given him, laden with obscure Italian history and all that gloomy antisemitism. Just the thing to briefly glance up from, perhaps nod, he reminded himself, then instantly return to. Maybe flash the cover as a reminder to maintain the appropriate social buffer zone.

"Oh I loved that book! He is a master!" the woman exclaimed with her smile, and then went on to offer what he had to admit were pretty good insights about the thing. She had settled in and, he noticed, did not remove anything to read or do as the plane took off. "So what do you do, J.?" she asked before he even realized she had somehow extracted his name—he preferred to go simply by his first initial—from him.

What did he do ... Amazing how she cut right to the quick. But then again, as Debra had recently pointed out, it seemed like everything lately was the quick for him. "Look," she said, reading the definition online, "'the quick' is any area of living flesh that is highly sensitive to pain or touch. That's like the perfect metaphor for you. I say 'good morning' to you and you wince."

"I can't help it if I am 'highly sensitive' to lies and misrepresentation."

"What?"

"'Good' morning."

Debra sort of smiled, but then looked more closely at him. "And why are you wincing now?"

"Also highly sensitive," he conceded, "to the truth."

The truth was, of course, that there was nothing wrong with being a physician, and a reasonably successful one—even if he was losing faith in the contemporary practice of medicine, was painfully aware that every patient ended up deceased no matter how he treated them, and even more painfully aware that he had already crossed the hump of his own life and was very much on the descent. Yes, something was surely off lately, more than just lately, a couple of years already, at least since the tragic passing of his college friend, maybe even longer. His gentle demeanor had developed rougher edges; his great capacity for compassion was declining; his once legendary sense of humor was becoming, how did Debra put it, more mythical. He was officially forbidden from engaging in what-iffery by his wife. And yet—

What did he do? The truth was, he didn't know what he was doing.

With these thoughts in mind he returned to Brenda O'Brien (for she had shared her name), and made another effort to assert his misanthropy. "I'm a philosopher," he stated matter-of-factly, wondering how someone so sensitive to misrepresentation had gotten so comfortable with the lying.

Not *fully* comfortable exactly, still not yet, saying this. It seemed pompous to call yourself a philosopher. And if there was one thing he wasn't, it was pompous, although he did wonder whether it was pompous to deny one's own pomposity. But anyway, he reminded himself, the pomposity was good since the whole *point* was to repel, to solicit the glazed eyes and disinterested "oh," the turning away so that he could return (in this case) to the Eco novel—which despite (or perhaps because of) the heavy history and gloomy antisemitism was in fact rather compelling.

But not this time.

"A philosopher!" his new friend Brenda exclaimed, her eyes twinkling.

He groaned silently, realizing it was probably too late to go to Debra's plan B and pretend he was deaf. Plan C, start speaking in tongues, maybe? Speaking in tongues, what an interesting expression, he thought. *Glossolalia* was the—

"So tell me," Brenda had continued, oblivious to the anxious expression on his face, "what are some of your sayings?"

His sayings?

"I'm sorry?" he said, wondering if that qualified.

"Ha!" she laughed. "One of our philosophy professors had someone ask him that on a plane recently. Isn't that delightful? But then I thought, why not? I am always looking for pithy ways of putting things, short, sharp insights. We are actually quite fond of slogans, you know. A word in time saves nine, and all that. And so I meet a philosopher, and I ask, what are some of your sayings. You never know, right?"

You never do know, he thought.

He who had in fact been reading some philosophy recently and over the years, with his already ancient interest in art history, in gargoyles, in tenebrism. With his dabbles into the history of medicine, a history which really was a long series of *philosophical* errors from olden times up until the very conference he was en route to attend. With his near obsession in recent years with the artistic representation of corpses, executions, dissections. He who between practicing medicine and reading everything by Eco and co-managing the three overgrown monsters who were their teenaged children had scribbled some three hundred pages about Rembrandt's famous *The Anatomy Lesson of Dr. Nicolaes Tulp*, and still hadn't gotten much beyond the cadaver's unflayed right hand. He who had even written a novel himself a hundred years back, maybe already then trying to fill the void threatening, like a black hole, to suck up everything around it. It had simply never occurred to him that actual philosophers, who wrote all those articles and spoke at all those conferences and taught all those students, who apparently had something to say, should therefore have, you know, *sayings*.

And shouldn't he—pretending to be one such philosopher?

In his head J. started running through some possibilities. "Never listen to a philosopher!" came immediately to mind. No; too annoyingly clever. "Follow your heart." Too cloyingly cliché. "Every choice presents two options, the one we choose, and the one we instantly regret not having chosen." Too—close to home. Some profundity? "God exists or not, and either way the implications are staggering." Too damn profound. "Whereof one cannot speak, thereof one must be silent"—perfect, if only someone (he thought Wittgenstein) hadn't already said it. Tear down the wall: Pink Floyd and Ronald Reagan. I have a dream. All you need is love. Happiness is a warm puppy. All taken! What if, he asked himself, in a final desperate shot, the Hokey-Pokey *is* what it's all about?

He had nothing.

He found himself experiencing a new sensation: he was actually speechless.

Unfortunately Brenda did not suffer from that problem. "That is *so* fascinating," she said enthusiastically, breaking into the cocoa-tinged cardboard sticks the airline passed for chocolate. "You studied gargoyles in college? I *love* them. And I have never heard of 'fugitive sheets.' What was that word—eco-, ecor—?"

"'*Ecorché*,'" J. said again quietly.

"And you have written an entire book about that single

painting? It sounds so gruesome, and *so* fascinating. How lucky am I, to get such an interesting seatmate! I have many questions for you, Doctor. And the timing. It's perfect. Uncanny, really. You know, I am having another one of my simply crazy ideas ..."

Maybe Brenda O'Brien was not so dreadful after all, J. found himself thinking some time later. She was awfully enthusiastic, true, but in this case her enthusiasm was about him. And maybe he could do with a little enthusiasm about himself. The attempts at misanthropy required just so much effort, what with his continual backsliding into, what, *philanthropy* was not quite the word, but still, he supposed. And his long hours studying Dr. Tulp, staring at the man, staring at the strange off-center gazes of the pointy-bearded associates, wondering just who or what were they all looking at, or for, as if they were aware of someone, or something, a witness, a point, a purpose. There was no masking the fact that he felt tired, lately, so deeply tired, of his job, of his surly monsters, maybe even Debra with her ever-penetrating eyes directed at him—

By the end of the flight he found himself giving this woman in the heavy bubble-themed sweater a longer look—a little awkward, trapped in their seats with their faces only maybe two feet apart—and also found himself if not, well, enthusiastic, then at least entertained by, and entertaining, her proposition.

2

THIS IS DEFINITELY A terrible idea, J. was thinking three days later in the back seat of the car, some fifty minutes and God knows how many small winding roads into having no idea where he was or where, exactly, he was going. "Are you sure this is the right way?"

"Are you sure you have to ask that every five minutes?" the driver replied in a gently lisped monotone that at least was a break from the grunting comprising the driver's conversation to this point.

And five minutes was actually pretty good, J. thought, considering that he was worrying about it every two. In between he kept himself busy with the equally vexing question of just what sex the driver was. Discreet glances revealed nothing definitive: the medium-length hair, the neutral-pitched voice with the moderate lisp, the posture, the smooth face that maybe suggested the feminine until you looked more closely and saw some light make-up maybe covering a very closely shaven beard.

Well, it was none of his concern, J. thought—the driver's sex or whether this was the right direction. He turned his attention to the scenery, which had turned from light woods into deepening forest. He had never been in this part of the country before, didn't realize how thick the forests were, the old growth. He was beset by a sense of foreboding, feeling a little overheated, even—

"So," he said, *not* asking whether they were going the right way, "how long have you been driving for the college?"

"Since I started there."

"Ah! You—were a student?"

"I still am."

"Oh," J. realized that in addition to being sex-ambiguous the driver was also age-ambiguous. "What year are you, then? Junior? Senior?"

"They don't do 'junior' and 'senior' there."

"Oh? So, how do you measure progress, then?"

"They don't do 'progress' either. They don't like to measure."

"Then, what? How do you—when do you—graduate?"

"You do classes, if you want. You ripen. You leave. Or not."

"You ripen?" J. asked, after a short deliberation on just which component of that strange answer to pursue first.

The driver seemed to grunt, a deep-throated sound with a hint, J. thought, of the masculine. He was just about to ask if they were going the right way when the car slowed and stopped.

"Choose," the driver commanded.

J. looked out the window. Through the deepening shadows of the forest he saw they were at a fork in the road.

"What's that?" He pointed at the statue in the middle of the fork. A good fifteen feet tall, a Native American warrior. That it was not a symbol of universal brotherhood was evidenced by the menacing expression on its face and the half-dozen scalps it was holding by a short cord.

"Little Chief."

J. didn't feel inclined to ask whether there was also, some-where, a Big Chief. "I don't understand. You want me to choose which fork to take?"

"If … you … dare," the driver said ominously.

"Is that a—joke?"

The driver grunted ambiguously.

"I don't understand," J. insisted. "You're the driver."

"My job is to take the passenger where he wants to go."

"But I don't know where I am going."

"That is your problem."

"Fine, left fork," J. said, then instantly changed his mind.

"No, right fork!"

"Left fork it is," the driver said as they resumed driving into the woods. "Just so you know, all ways lead to the asylum. Be at the bay in about fifteen minutes."

J. shook his head, feeling suddenly cold. It was beginning to get dark. He rubbed his arms and his body, again glad he had worn his jacket on the plane so it hadn't disappeared with his luggage. He pulled out his phone and checked the time. They were good. Forty-five minutes until the evening ferry. Don't miss it, Brenda had warned, because the next one isn't until morning and you'll miss your talk. He thought maybe it would be a good time to call Debra. True, she didn't need to know where he was at every moment. A couple of years back she had suggested he install a GPS chip in his body so she could continuously monitor his whereabouts. He enjoyed this pleasant banter until, a short while later, she explained to him that in fact she was being sarcastic and they were bickering. For a moment he wondered if they were turning into his parents.

All ways lead to the asylum—hey, that was pretty good.

"Sorry," the driver explained in the lispy monotone a few moments later. "We just entered the dead zone at the fork. Satellite, cell phone service, spotty at best. Largest spot on the national map like that."

J. put away his phone, glad in a way that he had been unable to make the call. "You folks," he was thinking about the long drive through endless forest and the island toward which he was now headed, "are pretty remote out here. How does the college function? Without—communications?"

"There's a cable," the driver said as the bay came into view and they pulled into a parking lot next to the sign for the *Grand Island Ferry*. "Connects to the mainland. And the grid. For those who want to be connected. But for most—"

"Yes?"

"What happens on the island stays on the island."

The island, J. thought, and would have smiled if not for the eerie feeling at the coincidental reference. Still it sounded appealing, to disconnect from the mainland. Had its virtues, he thought, getting out of the car, taking in the splendid view: the red-orange sun just dipping into the watery horizon, the island on which the college was housed visible way out there, the fall chill invigorating even with his jacket on. A wooden sign near the dock simply stated *Nevergreen*. Maybe he should just buy himself a one-way ticket ...

J. started toward the boat, the ferry.

This is a terrible idea, he found himself thinking.

He didn't know this Brenda woman at all. And why had she darted off so quickly after they landed, after having been so friendly during the flight? And who did he think he was, to go to an actual college, and speak to an actual audience? Yes, he had written some three hundred pages about that painting, but what he hadn't mentioned was the amount of space in those pages dedicated to doodles of skulls and skeletons.

"Of course you should do it," Debra had said when he called her from the airport, waiting for his luggage not to arrive. "Your whole death and dissection thing. You have actually been asked to speak about it. Rather than be asked to stop speaking about it."

True enough. "And yet—"

"Enough with the 'and yets,' doc. What was that podcast line you liked so much a couple years ago? 'In the long clusterfuck of sorrow which is an average human life, we have only—' —what is it, 'fifty-four hundred—'"

"Forty-five."

"'Forty-five hundred hours, to do something worthwhile.' And here this woman appears, this assistant you think to the president of some college who has a last-minute speaker cancellation to deal with, who offers you a few valuable hours to talk about something you love, which just happens to be perfectly suited for the season. It's like the stars are aligning for you, and you want to turn them down?"

"The guy who said that line committed suicide," J. noted.

"All the more so."

"I would have to extend my trip another couple of days."

"A little time apart is healthy for a relationship, you know."

J. sighed. "I would also have to skip the last day of the conference."

"You mean the mind-numbing and soul-destroying conference you attend only for the required continuing education credits, that brings you up to date on the latest techniques you do not actually use in your work?"

"That would be the one."

"Listen, doc," Debra said, her voice softening. "You don't need to worry, we can manage here. Just go. And enjoy your several worthwhile hours at the—what did the woman call it?"

"Don't fall off the ferry," the driver's lisp penetrated his evening-dream, "the piranhas are hungry this time of day."

"Is that a joke—" J. started to say when someone ran into him nearly full-force and knocked him over to the side of the path.

The driver helped J. to his feet.

"What the hell was that?" J. brushed himself off.

The driver pointed back to the parking lot, where the one rather disheveled passenger coming off the incoming evening ferry had raced into her car and was high-tailing it out of there.

The driver shrugged. "Keeping it crazy, I guess."

3

"Welcome to the asylum, Dr. Jeffrey!"

Brenda, wearing the same bubble sweater from the plane, was waving from the illuminated dock as he disembarked unsteadily from the longest thirty minutes of his life. The bay may have looked serene on boarding, with the sun sinking into its pristine surface, but underneath it was home to criss-crossing currents that made for some not smooth sailing. These famous undertows in fact made the island the ideal location for The Nevergreen Asylum for the Lunatic, Imbecile, and Idiot when it was established in 1821—or so said the tourist brochure on the boat. As the institution's marketing materials boasted at the time, no one committed there ever left; a boast as much about their dedication to lifelong care as about the impossibility of escaping. Not that anyone even in their right mind would want to leave, since the place was beautiful: plenty of woods, surrounded by water, and lots of wildlife, including a rare species of miniature pig initially introduced to control the infamous fungal infestation of 1823. When the necrophilia scandals, and more importantly the subsequent lawsuits, finally *did* destroy the institution soon after the infamous insect infestation of 1921, the real estate was promptly snapped up by some visionary investors who wanted to found a new sort of private college. The Nevergreen College was born—still referred to, by townies and gownies alike, as "the asylum." The students in particular had long embraced the informal motto, "Keep It Crazy."

"How are you, Doctor?" Brenda took his extended hand. "Do

you—" she peered compassionately at his complexion—"need to vomit?" She gestured to a cordoned-off area near the end of the dock, softly lit. "That is a popular spot."

"I'm good," J. lied as he gratefully settled on solid land.

"Then let us follow the guidestones, friend," Brenda said as she led the way to a paved path through the darkened trees, gently illuminated by small, rounded lamps on the ground that looked like glowing stones. Vehicles were not permitted on the island, she explained, so everyone walked everywhere, along paths guided at night by these gorgeous smooth stones donated by an alum. It was a good thing he didn't have any luggage because she had forgotten to bring a wagon! "Watch your step," she warned as he nearly placed his foot in a mound of red fibrous droppings.

"That was close," he said.

"No, you're supposed to step *in* the pig droppings. It's good luck," Brenda explained cheerfully. "Ah well, bad luck for you then!"

By now J.'s seasick-nausea had been replaced by an indistinguishable nervousness-nausea. Generally speaking he did not like being in the dark, metaphorically or literally, and here he was both, following flickering lights through nocturnal woods populated by ravenous carnivorous pigs. Okay, he added the ravenous carnivorous part, but still. And he was on his way to giving a lecture to real academics, to people who had taken his path not taken, to people Debra believed often displayed their own peculiar forms of mental illness, and she should know, she pointed out, as a professional psychologist and as the daughter of one such academic. Her dreadful narcissist father with his years-long fixation on that seventeenth-century natural philosopher Igno-something—

"Ravenous and carnivorous! You have a wonderful imagination, Doctor," Brenda was saying. "Don't worry, almost no one ever sees them. We just find their droppings here and there. Ah, here we are. The Overlook!"

As they came into a clearing there was a modest block-like

stone building with enough lights on to make it look reasonably warm, welcoming, safe. It was the first building constructed for the asylum, Brenda noted, pointing next to the front doors to the foundation stone in which the year 1820 was carved, originally housing the medical staff whose job it was to watch over the inmates, hence the name. When the takeover occurred now almost a century ago it was converted into a guesthouse.

"It's awfully large, no?" J. followed her past an unstaffed front desk then down one of the dreary corridors leading from the lobby. "For the college?"

"Thirty-five rooms!" Brenda concurred. "There used to be lots of tourists."

"Really?"

"Sure! The asylum. Very rich history here. Speaking of which, you must visit our Museum of Curiosities while you're here, which documents it. And the college itself, of course, with our own reputation. And the wildlife. People hope they will see the little piggies. There's a gift shop on campus where you can purchase a jar of preserved droppings if you like."

"But—used to be? Tourists?"

Brenda hesitated as they came to the door of his room, seemed to brush something off the handle. "Well," she dug through her bag for the key, "it has fallen off some. There was," she hesitated again, "well, an episode. A few years back. Tourists just come for the day now instead of staying over."

"An episode?"

"Ah! Found it. Come on in. It may not be the Ritz, but I hope you will find it adequate."

Definitely not the Ritz. Some peeling wallpaper, a cobweb or two more than necessary, perhaps could use a more thorough dusting—he imagined Debra's mother pulling a second pair of white gloves over her white gloves before inspecting the room—but the place was adequate, heated, with a functioning if dim 60-watt bulb in the bedside lamp.

And quiet.

"Is anyone else staying here?" J. was suddenly aware of thirty-four cobwebbed empty rooms around him and the abandoned front desk.

"It's all yours, friend! Do you need to freshen up a little before dinner? It's—" Brenda checked her watch, "6:50. I've asked some lovely friends to join us at 7:15. Your talk is at 8:30. Will that be all right with you?"

"Well, no luggage, so nothing to unpack. I would like to maybe—wash up. Is there somewhere …?"

"Of course! There should be toiletries at the front desk. Just help yourself."

"There's no one working here?"

"Well, unfortunately, no," she frowned, choosing not to mention the Board of Elders' across-the-board cutting of all non-administrative budgets.

"You're not worried about people, students, stealing the toiletries?"

She brightened. "Not at all! We're big on the honor system here."

"Ah," he added, remembering what the driver had said, "and is there internet here? Cell service?"

"Ha!" Brenda exclaimed, then added, as if proudly, "Largest satellite dead spot in the country! But nevertheless, while there may have once been barbarity on this island today we are quite civilized. Thanks to our special cable there is wi-fi covering most of the island, and cell service through the network. I shall write down the password."

A few minutes later J. was washing his face (having run the water to let the rust drain out), resisting the urge to call his wife who did not need to know where he was at every moment, and reminding himself to ask again about the "episode" that Brenda had referred to.

4

"FRIEND J., EVERYONE! Everyone, friend J.!"

Everyone was five in number. Four of them rose to greet him as Brenda led him from the buffet to the table in what had been the Splenda Faculty Dining Room until the college awoke to the many problems with that name. First to go was the "Splenda," once it became clear that Big Food's malevolent money had no home in a place of higher virtue. Then it also became clear that it was wrong to nominally segregate and privilege the faculty, but less clear what to do about it. After a long, bitter, and eventually inconclusive attempt to rename the space it was now simply known as the Former Splenda Faculty Dining Room; and while it was officially open to all, most students boycotted it because of its history of anti-studentism, as did most faculty members, in solidarity with the students.

That included Orlanda Gan, a professor of art history who responded to J.'s extended hand by declaring, in a vaguely British accent, "I hereby register my objection to our meeting in this space," then quickly sitting down to protest the hierarchical custom of standing up to meet a new person. She had only agreed to come as a favor to Brenda, who had more or less begged her, as an art historian, to attend the dinner.

J. dropped his unshaken hand to his side.

Robert Merritt, a mathematics professor wearing a corduroy jacket with elbow patches, a tightly knotted bowtie, and a neatly trimmed graying beard, sighed loudly. "Orlanda objects to many things," he explained, beckoning for J.'s hand, which he shook

17

vigorously. "Thanks to the beautiful thing which is tenure, I, personally, am able to be in favor of everything she objects to."

"You are such an arse, Robert," Orlanda snapped.

"Like that," Robert continued. "She can't even just say 'ass' like everyone else. She's from rural Ohio. I'm pretty sure they don't say 'arse' in Cuyahoga County."

"These two," Brenda smiled uncomfortably.

"Don't make me intervene," a small woman introduced as "Peace" said in a tone somewhere between supportive and threatening. It was possible she was joking, as she was also introduced as a professor of conflict studies. What was not explained was whether she had chosen the field because of the name, or vice versa.

"They've been squabbling ever since they divorced," Luiz Bacharo whispered into J.'s ear, the long, hip hair on his young head tumbling into J.'s lap. Friend Luiz was a Vice Dean in the Department of Community Values—although the phrase "Vice Dean" was frowned upon because "Vice" was the opposite of "Virtue," which it was the Department's main priority to promote, so for a while he was known instead as the Virtue Dean, until it was also realized that "Dean" implied a privileged status incompatible with the fundamental value of equality it was also the Department's main priority to promote. J. was so busy working this out that he didn't even wonder about the fact that there was an entire "Department of Community Values" at the college.

"When was that?" J. whispered back.

"Thirteen years ago."

J. shuddered any time anyone even mentioned divorce. "And this is…?" he nodded toward the larger, rounder, older, bald gentleman at the table in the wheelchair who had (obviously) not risen with the rest of them on J.'s arrival nor greeted him, and who had silently allowed a young man personal assistant to serve him from the buffet.

"I present," Brenda whispered, "Dr. Taslitz M. Fester."

"Formerly of the Department of Conspiracy Studies," Luiz

whispered. "Currently College Professor At-Large."

"Large Professor At-Large," Robert added loudly.

"Barbarian," Orlanda hissed at Robert.

"And what is a Professor At-Large?" J. poked around his plate with his fork, not confident he could identify all the food items there.

"He is no longer affiliated with any department," Brenda explained.

"That's because he doesn't actually teach," Robert added. "Which is not surprising, because he also doesn't speak."

"Six years of silence, and counting!" Luiz affirmed proudly. "But you overlook his annual honors seminar, friend Robert. It's called 'The Sound of Silence,'" he turned to J., "and advanced students simply clamor to take it."

"Of course they do," Robert said. "Fourteen weeks around a seminar table with no one saying a word. I'm sure it's very cathartic. The occasional gurgle aside, and his annual howl, not a sound from the fellow."

"Robert does enjoy his tenure," Brenda smiled uncomfortably.

"Don't we all," Robert straightened his bowtie and nodded toward Dr. Fester. "Especially him. The students used to call him 'Big Chief' until they decided that 'Chief' was too hierarchical and 'Big' was too descriptive." He turned to the man and echoed his colleagues' reverential whisper. "How you doin' over there, Big Chief?"

"What Professor I-Am-A-Resentful-And-Envious-Medio-cre-Scholar is trying to say," Peace interrupted sternly, "is that Dr. Fester is a legendary polymath. He published more than two dozen books in almost as many fields before his magnum opus, *Humour and Pus*, when he stopped communicating. Absolutely groundbreaking material. *The Spread of Senescence* revolutionized epidemiology and public health. *A Pretty Nice Rooster To Be Around* changed the genre of memoir forever. And do not even trigger me on his three-volume *Homer Was A Woman*, which, happily, marked the beginning of the end for decrepit classics departments everywhere, particularly here. The man doesn't need to speak. His writings speak for him."

"Do they say 'hello' for him?" Robert asked. "'Good morning'? 'I'm sorry to hear about your surgery, how are you?'"

"They do for arses like you," Orlanda hissed.

J. was caught between his desire to absorb every word—Debra would want a full recounting on his return—and his discomfort with the fuzzy line between the academic and the personal. We pretend to teach and they pretend to learn, he thought, paraphrasing something from somewhere. "'The Spread of Senescence'?" he inquired to change the subject, and because it sounded interesting.

"Yes!" Brenda was equally eager for a subject change. "Dr. Fester exposed Big Medicine's suppression of the fact that aging is actually a contagious disease, due to an undetectable virus we spread through our saliva and sweat. That completely changes the way one conceives of the elderly!"

"And more importantly the young as well," Luiz twirled his long hair, "that is, the uninfected young. It required nothing less than a revaluation of values. A virtual reboot of our community value system here."

"Didn't you say," J. remembered, "that you have a whole Department of Community Values here?"

Luiz nodded. "We take values seriously here. We value values."

"Luiz is too modest to mention it," Brenda added, "but he was of *such* assistance to friend Sora in devising the Virtue Code for which we are so widely known!"

"Well, it really was a community effort," Luiz protested, "as it had to be, since it reflects, and disseminates, our community values. We can't do without anyone here, after all. I mean friend Sora was definitely part of it. But so was I. And others."

"That's Sora Rava," Orlanda piped in to explain. "Dean of Community Values."

"Luiz's boss, if you're taking notes," Robert explained further.

"But we prefer not to use the word 'boss,'" Orlanda glared at

Robert, "or the title 'Dean' for that matter."

"Big Sister, then," Robert offered.

"Robert," Peace said sternly, slightly rising in her seat. J. noticed that despite being small, Peace had some significant muscles.

"He's doing it again!" Orlanda protested.

"What?" Robert feigned innocence.

"That—that face. That expression. I'm reporting it."

"Orlanda," Brenda said with as much patience as she could muster. She was upset with herself for inviting them both, but it was always so difficult to get faculty to come to these dinners—even more so since the cuts to the non-administrative food service budget—and she wanted a respectable turnout. And she thought they had worked things out a little better since Orlanda had resumed taking her lithium. "The Face Offense ordinance was only approved last week. It doesn't become part of the Virtue Code until next semester. Speaking of which," she turned back to J., attempting to get back on track, "the Virtue Code has become a real tradition at Nevergreen. Every student signs it upon matriculation. And re-signs it in a ceremony at the opening of every academic year."

"One of my students even put it to music last year," Peace added proudly. "At tomorrow's gathering we're voting to make it our official solidarity hymn. Finally replacing that offensive alma mater. 'Nevergreen, How Proud We Are Of Thee'! How shameful. Can you imagine a more self-centered, egoistic alma mater than that? Thank Wicca times have changed."

"Wicca!" Robert muttered. "Next she'll be claiming that—"

"Speaking of change," Brenda quickly interrupted, rising, "Shall we show our distinguished guest the new vegan dessert buffet?"

"So the whole campus is vegan, then," J. said as he picked through an egg-milk-butter-sugar-gluten-flavor-free fake-chocolate item that was the best dessert available for the decimated budget. He willed himself to remember every detail about the food, because Debra would want a full recounting of that too later.

"As of next semester, officially," Luiz said. "The proposal just recently passed at the gathering and the student council."

"Long overdue," Peace added with another puff of pride, despite her earlier shame at being proud. The vegan resolution was her initiative, motivated by her work showing that most global conflicts were ultimately either about, or related to, or perpetrated by people inclined toward the use of animals for food. "One small instance where the plant-eating forces of truth and justice were victorious over the evil eaters of meat."

"Should a person named 'Peace' even be taking sides in a dispute?" Robert wondered aloud. "Asking for a friend."

"Perhaps not where there *are* two legitimate sides," Peace answered stiffly. "But that's not the case here. The truth is clear."

"Of all the ridiculous things I've heard on this campus, that is possibly the most ridiculous. Next you'll be claiming that the high price of housing contributes to the problem of global homelessness."

Peace ignored this dig at her first book. "But the data show it, Robert. Read my new book. Take any one of the—"

"I know your narrative. You cherry-pick some examples. Provide vaguely defined concepts and fit them to your data. You reach pre-determined conclusions. Q.E.D."

"That is false. And offensive." Peace's muscles were starting to bulge. "You can reject the empirical analysis, if you want. Look just at the values, even on this campus. Consider the Virtue—"

"Also ridiculous."

"Hardly! It's the highest display of our values. Ever since the Ep—"

"R-i-d-i-c-u-l-o-u-s," Robert spelled out.

"We are very committed to viewpoint diversity here," Brenda forced a weak smile as she looked at J., who was beginning to worry if his own face were committing a Face Offense.

"Let her friggin' speak!" Orlanda snapped, Cuyahoga briefly escaping.

"Thank you, Orlanda," Peace acknowledged. "As I was

saying—the Virtue Code—A community expresses itself in its choice to—"

"It's fascism," Robert interrupted again. "An expression of this community's fascist values. At least since The Episode."

"Let her speak, Robert," Luiz chimed in.

Peace persisted. "The sanctity of life cannot be equated with—"

"*Your* conception of the sanctity of life, you mean."

"The sanctity of life cannot be equated with—"

"*Your* conception of equation!"

"Let her finish, you beast!" Orlanda growled, as if lithium-free.

"Please, Robert," Brenda urged.

"All we are saying," Luiz pleaded, "is give Peace a chance."

Everyone stopped to look at him.

"I mean to make her point," Luiz said.

Robert raised his hands. "Fine. I yield."

"No," Peace answered, "I yield, to your privilege."

There was a long pause at the table that was only briefly interrupted by Brenda saying, again, "We are very committed to viewpoint diversity here," which in turn was followed by another long pause, until J. couldn't take his discomfort any longer and broke in.

"The Episode?" he asked.

There was a gurgle at the end of the table.

"Big Chief finally speaks!" Robert clapped his hands as all eyes turned to Dr. Fester, who remained staring straight ahead and made no further sound. "Touch of indigestion there, Big Fella?"

"It was nothing," Brenda answered J., ignoring Robert. "And it's past. So now, friend J., we are all excited about your talk this evening. It sounds so fascinating, and so in the spirit of the date. Can you give us something of a preview?"

5

"Okay, so it's a little underwhelming," Robert noted.

"You think?" J. said.

From his podium at the bottom of the amphitheater J. looked up and around the room. It was a lovely, comfortable auditorium used for their more prestigious visiting lecturers, who the last-minute cancellation for whom J. was substituting would have been. Aptly called "The Bubble Chamber," and clearly the inspiration for the sweater Brenda seemed constantly to wear, its walls depicted bubbles of many sizes, shapes, colors, floating, bouncing, rising, sinking, a perfect combination, J. briefly thought, of levity and gravity. Aptly also called "The Echo Chamber," its acoustics were as impressive as its aesthetics, and both as its capacity, with its some 450 seats.

Four hundred and forty-nine of which were empty.

"You think anyone will show up?" J. wondered aloud, not entirely sure what he was hoping for.

"Maybe," answered Robert from the front row. "Maybe not. Students, anyway, may be getting ready for tomorrow's full moon."

"What's to get ready for?"

"They do some sort of ritual at the Moondial."

"Moondial?"

"Like a sundial. But for the moon. Don't ask me how it works."

"All right. But what ritual? And why?"

"Don't ask me that either. Keeping it crazy, I think."

"And the faculty?"

Robert shrugged.

They waited a few minutes longer in silence.

"Shame our dinnermates couldn't make it," J. said.

They had each politely expressed regret about prior commit-ments, except, of course, for friend Fester, who had simply been wheeled away. Brenda in particular was embarrassed as she had set everything up, but she herself had some emergency sewing to do for the college (the budget cuts) and knew the talk was going to be a big success without her anyway. At least Orlanda had walked them over there, following the guidestones up the hill to the Adorno Center for the Fine Arts—named for the famous aes-theticist and critic of culture—since she did not trust Robert to show J. the Adorno monument that she had helped design, the "Adornment," in the wedge-shaped courtyard of the building.

"You will please notice," she said to J., since she would not speak to Robert, "the abstract manner in which the sculpture captures this great thinker's beautiful intellectual visage."

"Now *there's* some nonsense dressed up as sense," Robert said to J., since Orlanda had demanded he refrain from speaking to her as well. "You should also notice the concrete manner in which both it, and the man, are hideously ugly."

Rather than reply Orlanda had just added this to her long list of grievances against him and stormed off to her office, in the building, to stew over that list.

Robert shrugged. "Just as well. You would just have ended up offending them all. Never mind my ex-, all of whose various personalities get pissed off at the drop of a hat. Bacharo's hair grows every time he's piqued, which is why—well, you saw. And 'Peace' is the most divisive person you will ever meet. I think she works in conflict resolution because she starts so many. And I swear, she must file three or four OCs every day."

"OCs?"

"Offensiveness Complaints. She's probably filing one right now, because she believes I'm presently complaining about her."

"But you are."

"I'm not complaining. I'm simply stating the facts when I say she is a divisive, miserable excuse for a human being. I'm telling you, they should never have hired women faculty here."

"Really? Are you allowed to say—"

"Tenure," Robert said. "Now, what time are you scheduled for exactly?"

"Eight-thirty." J. glanced up and around the empty amphitheater, feeling a combination of nervousness, disappointment, and relief. "What should I do?"

"Ah, wait." There was a noise at the top of the auditorium, way up at the back. Two students had wandered in and seemed to be fiddling with something on the wall up there.

J. suddenly felt the same feelings but for the opposite reason. "Welcome," he said softly, the acoustics being such that they could hear him even way up there.

They looked down at him, somewhat glassy-eyed, almost feral-looking, J. thought, then turned on their heels and darted out of the room.

"Easy come, easy go," Robert said. "What the hell. Why don't you start?"

J. looked at Robert sitting expectantly, the neatly trimmed beard, the bowtie. A professor of mathematics, yes, but a genuine professor. You have finally been asked to speak, Debra had said, someone wanted to hear what he had to say, and he maybe did have something to say. It may only be an audience of one, he thought, but when you have something to say, one may just be enough.

Either that, or stay silent.

J. cleared his throat and began.

6

LIGHT WAS POURING IN through the little crack in the blinds he had neglected to close the night before, punishing him now by penetrating his closed eyelids like a hot screwdriver through cool brain. J. found himself emerging from an extraordinarily deep sleep, fighting upward through layers of consciousness, guided by that hot sharp light. He realized, as his eyes opened and then turned away from the glare, that he was extremely hungry. Last night's dinner had been unsatisfying as it was, and based on the growling in his stomach that must have been many hours ago.

That reminded him of the alarm clock. He glanced over at it. The red numerals, blinking, indicated 4:49 AM.

4:49 AM? he wondered as he emerged more fully into consciousness. That seemed inconsistent with—hot screwdriver of light penetrating cool brain. A pretty good image for someone mostly asleep, he thought. But the sun was up, doing its thing. So it couldn't be 4:49 AM.

The blinking lights.

The power had gone out.

Ah!

It hadn't been a dream. The thunder in the middle of the night. A sonic boom, startled him awake. Or he'd thought he was awake, since he woke into a blackness and silence so deep he was thinking he must be dreaming—at least until a blast of lightning illuminated the window. That's odd, he'd thought, when seconds had ticked by. Had he first heard the thunder, only to be followed by the lightning? But then he must have fallen asleep again because the next thing he was aware of was hot screw-driver cool brain.

And now here he was, in his room, at the Overlook. Had come back here on his own last night, following the stones, retracing the path back to the dining room then back to the guesthouse, after his lecture. How disappointing, and what a relief, that Robert had stood up as soon as he began talking, mouthed the words, "Sorry!" and "Kids!" while pointing at his watch, and followed those two strange students out. J. had found himself as alone in that spacious empty auditorium as he was now in the spacious empty guesthouse.

Might as well, he had thought, and resumed his lecture where he'd let off. At least there was no one there to ask him, as Debra had also noted, to stop speaking.

The power had gone out in the night, he thought again as he stood and stretched. That gave him a creepy feeling. The island was connected by that single cable to the grid, to electricity and internet and the wider world, and apparently that cable could go out sometimes.

It would be good to get out of here.

His phone.

It was 8:05 AM. He pulled open the blinds, appreciated the morning light more properly. He realized he didn't know the ferry schedule. It was a little early; he would wait a while before texting Brenda. He thought briefly about calling Debra, but then realized that with the time difference she would be at work and would be even more annoyed than she already would be by the fact of his calling at all. She didn't need a live feed on what he was up to, she had said that time, though she would be happy to subscribe to his monthly newsletter.

Was that banter, or bicker, he wondered. Such a fine line.

Maybe it was a bad idea to come here, he thought as he got into the shower (after letting the rusty water drain out), and was still thinking when he pulled on the same clothes he had been wearing the night before, and the preceding three days, since being parted from his luggage. He was also thinking this when he took a tissue from the packet he had taken from the front desk and crushed the large spider (if it *was* a spider) on the wall just above the bed, but wait—it was actually Debra who had encouraged him to come, remember, to stop waffling, to stop regretting, and accept the invitation. So if it was a bad idea it was *her* bad idea. He reached for his phone to inform her of this when he also remembered the time difference, her reminder that some space was good for a relationship, and her observation that his parents' constantly competing to point out each other's mistakes was not really that cute after all.

It would be good to get out of here, he was thinking as he brushed his teeth just a little too vigorously, drawing a drop of blood from his gum. Also good to get something to eat, he thought, his stomach growling.

And coffee.

Aiming for sustenance and departure, J. opened the door of the room and stepped into the corridor, not noticing the large not-a-spider on the doorframe above his head, and also not noticing the note that had been slipped under the door some time during the stormy night.

7

THE PATH FROM THE Overlook that won the coin toss soon took J. into some light woods filled with flowering bushes happily soaking in the late October morning sunshine that penetrated the canopy. Despite his need for coffee he stopped to take some photos for Debra, who, unlike him, was an aficionado of flowers and who, also unlike him, knew something about them. Ran in her family, the whole flower thing, he thought, rewarding himself with marriage capital for remembering things like that. The path soon came up to a large Native American wood statue. Like Little Chief on the drive out here it was a fierce warrior brandishing a sharp spear, only bigger. And newer, too, as if recently installed. Perhaps *this* was Big Chief, J. thought, remembering Robert's comment about friend Fester last night. Looked like he was hunting, the way he held the spear, poised to stick something. Or maybe guarding something, J. thought as he walked a few feet further and saw, roped off in the woods, a small clearing. Some dozen wooden signs were staked in the ground, indecipherable symbols. A burial ground, a cemetery, perhaps. For a moment he wondered what the Nevergreen Asylum had done with their dead, scandals aside. Nobody ever left the place, so presumably there was a more sizable cemetery somewhere?

It was so silent here, peaceful. The silence of the eternally silent. Interrupted only by the occasional whisper of the chilly autumn wind.

And the pressing need for coffee.

Pushing on, J. followed the path as it emerged into the sunlight alongside some tall waterlogged grasses, swaying in the breeze, identified by a sign as *Mellow Marsh*. A short distance around the marsh to another path leading up a small hill, J. soon came up and over the grassy knoll onto an enormous lawn surrounded by a cluster of unusually shaped buildings punctuated by smaller oblong square buildings, all connected by criss-crossing paths. The building on his left opened into the courtyard containing the Adornment, so this was where he had been last night. In the center of the lawn J. could see tall hedges, a garden perhaps, clearly an attraction of some sort because paths also led to it from every surrounding building. All ways lead to the asylum, the driver had said; well many of the ways *at* the asylum seemed to lead to this bushy thing. Maybe he would check it out later, if he couldn't get himself out of here first, but by all means only after coffee.

This was clearly the main campus, the "upper campus" someone mentioned last night, made sense given the hill he had just climbed. At an hour most students would consider ungodly—8:53 AM said his phone—it was mostly empty. There were a few strolling about, with backpacks, jeans, sweatshirts, a couple were smoking, looking—*normal*, J. thought. No feral glances like the two students who'd popped in, and out, of his lecture last night. Well maybe not entirely normal: there were two young women dragging mattresses down a path for some reason, and in another area there were three students oddly looking toward the ground, making strange faces and rude gestures and filming themselves as they did so. As J. approached them he saw they were directing these actions toward one of the guidestones there; and as he approached closer he could see a small camera in the stone, along with a little plaque that read, "See Something Say Something."

"So sorry to interrupt," J. said to the student making a middle-finger "fuck you" sign to the guidestone camera as his friend filmed him, "but is there a café somewhere around here?"

The student swiveled to point his middle finger over the hedges at the building at the opposite end of the—well, it wasn't the stereotypical college quadrangle, J. thought, counting the six larger buildings, but more like a—hexangle? "Quicker to go around that way," the student added, pointing the finger at a path around the hedges then back at the hedges. "Otherwise you will probably get lost in dat."

"That?" J. asked, pointing.

"No, dat."

"What?"

"We call it 'dat.'"

"You call what 'dat'?"

"That. The whole thing."

"What? What is that? Dat?"

But the student had already returned to the camera and now inserted the middle finger deeply into his nostril while his two friends snorted. Feeling a little uneasy J. followed the path around the hedges, noticing that a number of the guidestones along the way also had those little cameras and plaques.

"It's the library," answered the female student vaping lazily in front of the building when J. asked about its sign, *The Crown Depository*. "People say there are books somewhere in there, from back when there still were books."

"Is that a joke?" J. asked.

"See for yourself," she shrugged and returned to her vape.

Well if there were books they certainly weren't on the first floor. As J. walked through he saw a recreation room with pool tables, ping pong tables, foosball (he perked up), and video games, a large hall in which students were setting up booths, smaller lounges with couches and comfy chairs and pillows (one of which had a pansies theme, he noticed, giving himself marriage capital for recognizing the flower), a seating area stuffed with stuffed animals, an art gallery with prints of nature themes, and vending machines dispensing snacks and drinks almost everywhere. There was an "Information Desk" along the way as well, unstaffed due to budget cuts but with piles of brochures clearly designed for tourists, at which J. might have stopped had he not also seen a sign saying *Coffée Bar* with an arrow pointing further on.

Had he stopped he would have picked up the brochure explaining that this building had once served as the medical center for the Nevergreen Asylum: where treatment was administered, experiments were undertaken, and the many resulting bodies embalmed and stored for future study (hence the "Depository"). After the lawsuits were settled the Crown family, who had donated a mentally incapacitated son to the eugenics laboratory there, sought to reclaim the institution's reputation by donating the money to convert the building into a modern university library. The embalmed bodies were allegedly removed and replaced with books. The rumors that the bodies were still somewhere on the premises—along with the alleged "books"—remained current to the day.

Instead of learning this J. was learning that the latest frontier in body piercing was the rim of eyelids, from the young man with the 7-inch man-bun atop his head, with miniature diamonds sparkling from the base of his eyelashes, and wearing the apron with the words, *Coffée Bar*.

"Isn't that painful?" J. was transfixed by the sparkles as he gratefully received his large mug of coffee.

"Maximally. The studs scrape my eyeballs every time I blink."

"Then why do you do it?"

"Because I can."

"Is that really a reason?"

"Also because you can't."

He had a point, J. had to agree, as he took the first long draft from the life-affirming and for some reason reddish elixir here apparently called coffée—which he promptly spat back into the mug. "What is that?!"

The barista blinked at him, grimacing. "Coffée. You don't like?"

"Not—coffee?"

"Hardly, dude," the young man snorted. "It's pomo. Warmed."

"And what is pomo?"

"Extract of pomegranate seeds, molasses. There is some crazy formula. Take like 613 seeds, ferment them in molasses, add eye of newt. Boil, bubble."

"It's—disgusting. Just—*awry*."

"Acquired taste. Everyone drinks it here. It wakes you right up. If you want it cold, it comes out of the fountains."

J. made a mental note to pick up a bottle of water when he could. "Any chance I could just have some straight, you know, coffee?"

"Whoa, whoa." The barista's eyebrows scrunched around the pins inserted through them as he eyed the visitor suspiciously.

"What?"

"Is this some kind of trap?"

"What?"

"You with the Virtue Patrol?" The barista lifted his hand to a button on the counter, poised to press.

"I honestly don't know what you're talking about."

The barista pulled away from the button, his eyebrows gradually unscrunching. A look almost of compassion seemed to cross the young man's face. "Listen, dude. Why don't you just go."

"I take it that's a 'no' to the coffee?"

"Dude. Just. Go."

So go he did. Some thirty-two minutes later he was standing at the door of the Intersections Lounge debating whether to enter. Some of that time he had spent trying to memorize that pomo taste in his mouth, in order to describe it in detail to Debra later; more of that time was then spent trying to expunge the taste from his mouth by diluting it with swashes of the soy milk, then the almond milk, then the imported cacao creamer that collectively reflected the Agricultural Justice Committee's boycott of Big Dairy. Suffice to say that the taste remained unexpunged, and J. remained irritable. The only saving grace was the thought that Debra would appreciate the coffee calamity when he recounted it later.

The rest of the time was spent perusing the literature at the Information Desk, which also provided him with a campus map. This latter confirmed that the main buildings *were* oddly shaped: they reminded J. of the chomping monsters from the old

Pacman video game. It also confirmed that the upper campus was indeed a hexagon, as the six Pacman buildings, with their "open mouths" facing inward, created with strategically placed pathways an impression of two overlapping triangles, inverted relative to each other. Thus was the upper campus officially named "The Kanisza Triangles"—after the Italian benefactor whose semi-psychotic daughter was both the last inmate at the Nevergreen Asylum and the first student at the Nevergreen College—though everyone just called it the Hex. The Crown Depository, where J. now was, was Pacman 1 at the top of the triangle; the Adorno Center was Pacman 6 at the bottom; J. noticed that Pacman 4, just above and to the right of Pacman 6, was called the "Center for Community Priorities," which was probably where the Agricultural Justice Committee did its important work. The smaller oblong buildings between the Pacmans were student residences called "lodges," also numbered one through six but in a straightforward clockwise manner. Smack dab in the middle of the whole thing were the hedges, which, J. now saw, comprised "Solomon's Maze," to which that student had referred for some reason as "dat."

So oriented—or disoriented—and with nothing else to do (at least until Brenda returned the text he had sent inquiring about the ferry schedule), J. decided he may as well explore the "Student Clubs Expo" getting underway in the Intersections Lounge and see how the kids were keeping it crazy these days.

8

THE LOUNGE WAS A very large space whose comfy furniture had been pushed to the perimeter to make room for several dozen long tables and booths with signs and literature and banners. Students were milling about, staffing the booths, visiting them, in some cases objecting to them. Impressive extracurriculars for a smaller school, J. thought as he strolled through, but all leading to the same conclusion: times had changed in the three decades since he had been in college.

There were some familiar clubs: a student government association, a newspaper, music, drama, political clubs. Nor did it surprise him, given what he had been reading about campuses, that the student Democrats had many students around a double table while next to them was a single table at which one lonely student sat, over a sign reading "Student Republicans, Student Capitalists, and Pro-Life Students"—on which the relevant s's had been crossed out: Student Republicans, Capitalists, Pro-Life Students. To be accurate, though, the student explained when J. briefly stopped by, there was another group that also called itself the Pro-Life Club. But they were so obsessed with preserving all forms of life that they had gone from merely covering their mouths with masks to avoid accidentally inhaling insects to refusing to eat even plants to finally calling, as logic entailed they must, for the mass extinction by starvation of all human beings, for the benefit of all *other* forms of life.

"I'm not crazy like them, man," the student explained. "I just don't think that women should have any say in what happens with their bodies."

36

"Where is their table?" J. nodded, intrigued.

"Not here," the student answered. "They don't make it out much."

And so it went from there. There were tables for the Anxiety and Depression Clubs with healthy unhealthy crowds; one for the Empathy Club, with its neatly inked banner, "When An Individual Feels, A Community Reels." Clustered with these was the Differently Abled Club advocating for disability rights, J. learned when he stopped by, most recently for a wheelchair ramp for the school's high diving board. "It's for the principle, the principle of inclusion," the earnest young woman explained when J. asked whether any wheelchair-bound person were likely to actually use the diving board. Yet right next to this table was the "Actually Abled Club," staffed by a muscular young man whose steroid-bulging t-shirt bore the simple phrase, "Hexant 5." According to his grunts the club was running an "anti-ramp" campaign against not only the diving board ramp but all campus ramps in general. Someone had somehow thought it a good idea to locate these two groups next to each other, where their representatives were busy exchanging hostile glances.

That same person also put the Carnivores Club next to the PETA Club, and as J. passed their booths hostile glances were becoming hostile words about the new veganism policy, with several hovering students filming the dispute with their phones. Harmless enough, J. thought, as long as they don't get *those guys* involved—those guys being the frighteningly made up students at the Zombie Club table and the one, frighteningly *not*-made-up student at the Maniacal Ax-Killer Club maniacally brandishing an ax. Harder to read was the student sitting at the intersection of the two tables, behind the Zombiac Club sign: also rather built, he had gentle blue eyes behind the little round glasses on his zombie nose. You shouldn't judge people on appearances, J. could hear Debra reminding him. True, but here appearances, plus the signs endorsing zombie axe-slaughter, were at least a start. Busy thinking this J. skipped right by the Theater table, thus failing to learn about the pending staging of the late unpublished Pinter play, *An Emergency*.

There was a large pomo dispenser as J. turned the corner toward the next aisle. Yawning students were filling their water bottles under the sign either inviting or commanding, "Help Yourself! Remember: A Glass in Time Saves Nine." J. instead turned down the aisle to find the Revisionist History Club and the Conspiracy Club, staffed by students moving between the tables. Adjacent to them was a student secret society called Humour and Pus, not so secretly connected (apparently) with Dr. Taslitz Fester's book of that name. It occurred to J. that, with his own obsession with the history of medical malpractice and with his unhealthy (according to Debra) need to make people laugh, "humour" and "pus" neatly described both his occupation and his preoccupation.

Meanwhile the same wise organizer had also placed the Indigenous Peoples Club next to the Settler-Colonial Club, and as heated words were becoming pushes and shoves there, mutual headlocks were happening between the Marginalized Peoples Club and the Cultural Appropriation Club; some dispute about Halloween costumes and about the rather tasty looking Vietnamese sandwiches both parties were offering. A student dressed in a suit and tie—was that his costume?—was egging them on, and filming them. But for the headlocks, J. would gladly have snagged a sandwich.

Coffee, coffee, J. was lamenting as well as he turned to the final aisle and immediately wished he hadn't. Grouped together airing their many mutual grievances were the Only Black Lives Matter Club, the White Is A Color Too Club, the Ur-Nazi Club, the Jihadi Martyrs Club, and the DIT Club, for Diversity, Inclusion, and Tolerance. And there was one more: an empty table set up with flowers and burning candles as some kind of memorial, with only the mysterious slogan, "All You Need is Love."

"Fascinating!" a woman's voice said behind him. J. turned to find a middle-aged couple, the man snapping photos of the tables while the woman, who had made the comment, read from a tourist brochure. "It says here that Nevergreen is a real haven for the violent and racist demographic. Their commitment to full diversity and inclusion attracts those who feel unwelcome elsewhere."

"Beautiful!" her photographer husband admired. "The 'inclusion' folks really bring everyone together."

J. sighed, realizing that the presence of these tourists meant he must have missed the first ferry of the morning. "Yeah," he added, recalling Brenda's comment from last night. "The commitment to viewpoint diversity is so broad here that it supports those who reject viewpoint diversity. I understand Nevergreen is the only school in the country to employ affirmative action quotas for white supremacists. Speaking of which—" he turned to the young man at the table, "'Ur-Nazi'? What is that, exactly?"

"We deeply condemn the Neo-Nazi movement," said the young fellow, either costumed, or just dressed, in a vintage Nazi officer's uniform and with stylish pince-nez glasses on his strong Aryan nose. "We are the original real deal."

J. backed away as the couple took selfies with young Himmler obliging them with a salute. As he turned the corner and came back toward the center of the room he found a large circular table, staffed by a tall thin young woman with severe eyes that made him even uneasier than the genocidal pince-nez he had just left behind.

"And this is," he mustered the courage to approach, an expression of discomfort crossing his face as he felt a little indigestion, perhaps triggered by the, you know, Jihadis and Nazis and zombiacs, and the fact that he had missed his first chance out of here, "the student newspaper?" Over the table was a banner announcing *The Howler*, under which was the motto: "Impressions You Can Trust."

The student raised her eyes from her laptop to his face, then to his eyes, and burned a stare into them. J. was reminded of the remark a colleague had made years ago, when describing the first date he had had with his wife. "She looked at me," he said, "and her eyes literally burned a hole in my soul." All J. could think at the time was that this was a fascinating not-literal use of the word *literal*, because eyes could not literally burn a hole in a soul.

How wrong he was.

A look like that should be against the rules, he thought, withering from their penetration. A Face Offense if ever there were one, making him feel as if *he* were the criminal. He was almost relieved when instead of burning him to the ground she just pulled out a phone and snapped a picture of him. Okay, that was a little strange, but at least it interrupted her withering stare.

"Come with me," a scratchy voice whispered somewhere below J.'s ear, startling him as he felt a tug on his elbow. "*Now*, Doctor. You are in great danger here."

9

SHE WAS HUNGRY.

SHE WAS HUNGRY.

She was *so* hungry. She hated being hungry. She hated many things, true, but she especially hated being hungry. Well, not "hate." *Hate* was a word her therapist was trying to get her to use less, not just out loud but in her thoughts too. Except, it seemed to her, about hate itself, one should definitely hate *hate*; that was all right. She definitely did not like being hungry. She did not like many things, true, but she especially definitely did not like being hungry.

She should have gotten some breakfast before coming to the Expo today. She thought there would be snacks or something, but with the budget cuts, nothing. The same thing happened last year. She ought to learn, her therapist was always urging that. But learning was such hard work. And she didn't like hard work. Fortunately she often did not need to put in the work. She had such good instincts. She grasped things instantly, usually, and it was uncanny how accurate her instincts usually were. Impressions You Can Trust—that was her motto all the way back to high school, and she was pleased that the *Clarion* had adopted it as its motto. A change-maker, a maker of change, that's who she was, and *so much* needed changing. She was particularly pleased at the positive reception of her first editorial last month, as the newspaper's newly inaugurated Editor-in-Chief, renouncing the title of Editor-in-Chief. Almost as pleased as she was that, as its newly christened Campus Observer instead, she had obtained the paper's staff's participation in the new mandatory photoshop

41

workshops, to help the images dominating the paper's pages better convey their intended truths. And almost as pleased again as she was that the paper had adopted her name change to *The Howler*. How perfect that was, given the history of this place, the asylum, the moon rituals, the wolf man thing. The pain, the agony. Ginsburg, and truth. Dr. Fester. Perfect vehicle for her Campus Observations. The mirrored eye she would cast upon them all.

Damn, she was good.

These fairs, these expos; next on her list.

She hated—definitely did not like—these expos. So artificial. People should do stuff. But at the expo you didn't do stuff, you represented yourself as doing stuff. Go ahead and be a Nazi or a Christian, advocate for or against viewpoint diversity, for or against marshmallows if that's your thing, it's all good. But to sit at a table and proclaim yourself a heterosexual, or a progressive, seemed stupid. Or to solicit other people to join you in your thing seemed beside the point. Each person should do their own thing. What does it matter what other people did? She herself was a journalist, her job was to observe, to report her impressions. And her impression was that these expos were an opportunity for people to pretend and solicit rather than simply be and do. If the *Howler* weren't so woefully understaffed—this year's cuts had axed most of the work-study students—she wouldn't be here herself. As it was she was getting worn out writing most of the paper herself.

Damn, she was hungry. But what she needed, she realized, wasn't just food. She needed a story. A really good story. The imminent caterpillar thing, she couldn't care less. Gross, yes, but no depth, action, principles. True, there was plenty of tension on campus lately, with the costume debate, the mattress girls, that idiot trying to remove pomo from campus. But these were all local, small-scale, disputes between individuals. What she needed—what the *Howler* needed—was something bigger, universal, deep. Something to involve everyone, concern everyone, anger them. Shake this place up a bit, or maybe shake it down;

get things howling, scare a few more students up for the paper, help her, to help the *Howler*. Oh, that's good, she thought; she should just call *herself* The Howler, would make things simpler.

She glanced around the room, waiting for an impression. Her instincts, always good. Don't need research, investigation, when you have your instincts. That's what the paper's faculty advisor, Prof. Peace, always said. She'd had Corrie read Prof. Fester's incredible book on journalism, *War As Peace: On Weaponizing Conflict*, which taught that the key was to act fast, to get the story out. After all, tomorrow it may no longer be true. In fact it might not be true right now, but that hardly mattered, what mattered was the impression. What feelings did it convey. An individual feels, a community reels. Because feelings were true no matter what the so-called facts were. Facts were always in dispute, murky, unclear; invented, oppressive, while feelings were clear and authentic and liberating. Feelings were the only *real* facts, really. Feel it, write it, post it, viralize, repeat. She was thirsty, she realized, must refill her bottle. And *so* hungry, she realized. She should have eaten breakfast. She hated being hungry.

She looked back down at her screen, went to the paper's website, changed her title from "Campus Observer" to "The Howler" to see how it felt. *L'Howler, c'est moi*, she thought. She was just gazing at this on the screen, examining how it felt, determining her impression, when there it was, she could feel it, she could feel the external pressure.

It was hatred she felt.

No not hatred but the hating of *hate*—

"And this is the student newspaper?" the man interrupted her impression.

She looked up at him, looked at him, looked into him. Looked at that—that *face*. Slightly puffy, slightly haggard, bleary eyes, some days away from its last shave, if her therapist could only see this face, for what she saw was what she felt was what she knew, that that face, with its mildly but sinister contorted expression, that whatever was inside or behind that face, that whatever came out of it, that that face was—before the impression could fade she grabbed her phone and snapped a photo of *the face of hate*.

Perfect, she thought as the man was seemingly pulled away, for this morning's mandatory workshop.

And then, she also thought, returning to her screen in search of the website, for the Resistance.

PART II

YOU ARE IN GREAT DANGER HERE

10

"Now, Doctor. You are in great danger here."

J. turned to see at a very small man with disheveled white hair and a tattered vest standing behind him. As J. turned the man seemed to slide in order to remain behind him. J. turned more sharply in order to roughly face the man, who slid a little further to remain slightly to J.'s right.

"Could you stop doing that?" J. spluttered.

"No," the man moved further to the right.

J. sighed. "And how do you know who I am?"

"It is my business to know. Now come with me."

"Who are you?"

"Not here. Not safe. Come to my office."

Well, why not? J. thought as he followed the man through a door he hadn't noticed at the side of the lounge, relieved to leave the simmering tension of the Student Clubs Expo. The man looked harmless enough as they walked through the darkened corridor, with his diminutive size and the ragged tear down the back of the vest. Several turns down several darkened corridors—this place was bigger than he realized—and they passed another door quite toward the rear of the Depository.

"Emergency Exit," the man pointed to the words painted across it. "When you need to pull foot quick. Mark it, if you are wise."

"So marked," J. said despite having no idea what it was to "pull foot" as they turned down another corridor and arrived at an office door. On this door was a simple sign: "Librarian."

"You're a librarian," J. observed as the man pulled out a large wooden key.

"*The* librarian," the man said, clearly annoyed as he slipped the key into the door. "One might say 'The Librarian,' capital T, capital L. But it seems the definite article violates the Virtue Code in some way. So there you have it."

"So it remains this way—indefinitely?"

The man either didn't get J.'s attempt at humor or simply didn't find it funny, neither (as Debra had observed) being uncommon lately. "Have a seat, Doctor," he said as they entered the office, then gestured toward some liquor bottles on a shelf. "May I offer you a horn of something? A little anti-fogmatic, to clear the spirits, eh?"

J. glanced at the bottles, recognized none. Many small jars also lined the shelves, of quinine hydrochlor, vitriol, nitre, two bottles of Agua de Vilajuiga, most produced by a company called Burroughs Wellcome & Co. Was that—a jar of leeches? Turning back to the librarian J. noticed that the man's oversized desk was a mess, with papers piled everywhere and covered with half-eaten sandwiches and half-nibbled cookies and two half-glasses of milk. J. brushed some organic matter off the chair before the desk and obliged the librarian's command. "No, I'm good, thank you. Are you—you have an interest in the apothecarial arts?"

"You cannot be too careful around here, Doctor." The man stared at J. with bulging (J. couldn't *not* notice) proptosic eyes from beneath bushy white eyebrows as he took his own seat across the desk. Most of his body was obscured by the desk, just his head and shoulders visible. He lowered his voice, "How are things for you here? Doctor?"

"Oh, that's a good one," J. said, indicating the plaque on the desk that read, A *lunatic is a minority of one.*

"I asked you a question, Doctor."

"Ah, sorry. Right. Things are fine, it seems. Why? Should I— be worried about something?"

The man's eyes bulged. "I make it a rule never to trust

appearances, Doctor. Not even here, in this office," he added
with an extra air of mysteriousness.

"What? Why not?" J. glanced around again, the office seem-
ing to him a rather ordinary, if extraordinarily messy, place. Well
perhaps not entirely ordinary, with the leeches and all. And
that oddly shaped skull on the other shelf, some phrenological
artifact maybe. And that painting on the wall, slightly askew,
was familiar: dice players by candlelight, the play of light and
shadow, the details on the hands, the knuckles, reminiscent of
his Rembrandt, he ought to know this …

"I should not say," the librarian failed to explain.

"What? Why not?" J. asked again.

"I should not say that either. I have probably said too much
as it is."

"But you've hardly said anything so far. Not even your name,
in fact. Mr…?"

"I am The Librarian, as I told you. Is that not enough?"

As J. pondered this he noticed the nameplate on the desk half
obscured by a half-eaten sandwich. "So what can I do for you,
Librarian—Freinz, is it?"

Freinz frowned, annoyed. "Do for me? The question is what I
can do for you, Doctor."

"Okay. So what *can* you do for me?"

"In light of the circumstances, probably nothing."

"What circumstances?"

"The danger, Doctor!"

"What danger?"

"I have said too much."

"But you haven't said anything!"

"Exactly. You should not have come back here."

"But you took me here!"

"Did I, Doctor? Did I?" From beneath his bushy eyebrows Freinz's eyes bulged at him meaningfully. "You ignored my note."

"What note?"

"And now you deny it?"

"Deny what?!"

"Ah. The Department has gotten to you."

"What?"

"They deny everything. Now you deny everything. The connection is undeniable."

"What are you talking about? What department?"

"Must we continue to draw the long bow, here, Doctor? Eh? Are we not both speaking of," he dropped his voice, "Conspiracy Studies?"

J. shook his head. "There really is a Department of Conspiracy Studies here?"

Freinz gazed, bulged, analyzed. "Oh, you are good."

J. just stared back at him blankly. "Georges de la Tour," he suddenly said, recalling the painter's name.

The librarian looked at the painting, then looked at J. closely. He hesitated, then pulled a timepiece on a chain from his vest pocket. "Enough with the jibber-jabber. Now listen carefully. When it happens, you must return here. To me, and me alone. I shall stash you away somewhere. Until things blow over. May I count on you to return here, Doctor?"

"When what happens? What are you talking about?"

"When *it* happens, Doctor."

"What? What is 'it'?"

"The humour, Doctor," Freinz said softly. "And the pus."

J. just stared at him in exasperation.

The librarian stood up, which barely made a difference. "It is good we had this little talk, eh? If confronted, I will deny its occurrence and I suggest you do the same. And remember this: *trust no one.*"

"What? That's it? This is—over?" The strange little man had walked to the office door and opened it, and was gesturing for J. to leave.

"We have gone too long as it is, Doctor. Absquatulate!"

"What?"

"Shoo!"

J. peered at the man standing in the doorway waving his hands at him. Then his attention was drawn to the side of the door where he saw—could that be—a caterpillar crawling up the doorframe? J. shuddered. There was little more repulsive, he just hated creepy-crawlies ...

"Shoo! Shoo!" Freinz repeated urgently.

J. found himself outside the closed door, not at all sure what had just happened much less what was going to happen, when he felt a sharp jab in his back.

11

"Ah," Robert exclaimed. "I thought I might find you here."

"Did you have to jab me so hard?" J. rubbed his back.

"I did. You were pretty lost in thought there."

"Ah! It was the strangest thing. That man. There was a—"

"Tell me while we walk," Robert interrupted.

J. followed him through the corridors as Robert strode away. "What's the matter? Did something happen?"

"Have you seen the student newspaper today, by any chance?"

"No," J. worked to keep pace with him as they left the Depository onto the main campus. They came to a broad path that ran between a pair of prominent signs, the one the female students had been dragging their mattresses along earlier. The sign on the right bore the words *Walk of Fame*; the one on the left, *Walk of Shame*. J. pointed as they crossed over the path. "What are those about?"

"This path connects the two largest lodges in the Hex," Robert indicated the oblong buildings at the opposite ends of the path. "One and six, if you're taking notes. The students here are like bunnies on bennies. Get shook up with a hook up, they like to say. Before they abolished sports the jocks used to say bump, hump, and pump. Oh, and dump. I think it's something in the pomo. It perks them right up."

J. felt slightly repelled. "And the signs?"

"The walk you do the next morning. Fame or Shame, depending on your perspective. They installed extra security cameras in the stones there too, for good measure. See something, say something, you know. Ah, excuse me, please." Robert maneuvered them past and through several tourists clustered around a red smelly pile of droppings, snapping photos. "Bonanza! They got to see some pig shit."

Had he missed another ferry? J. wondered, momentarily overcome by the stench. He would text Brenda again as soon as he could. "So," he said, out of breath attempting to keep pace, "what is the story with that Freinz fellow? The librarian?"

"A real character. Allegedly descends from a long line of librarians. More likely from a long line of inmates at the asylum."

"He seemed to think I was in danger."

Robert stopped walking for a moment. "He's a good librarian. And he seems to always know what's going on on campus. But he's a little—he's a character. You'll probably be fine."

"Probably fine? What does that mean?"

"Come, we'll discuss it at Aaliyah's office. We're almost there. Hexant 4, if you're taking notes. Just around the Maze here." Robert quickened his step as J. struggled to do the same.

"Who," he breathed, "is Aaliyah?"

"The Vice President. If we still used that title. Now we just call her 'friend Aaliyah.' Here we are. The Center for Community Priorities." Robert gestured upwards as they arrived at the base of the tallest Pacman building. "Administrative building, also known as the Castle, the Hive, and of course—" he gestured upward again, "the Big Dick. Bottom three floors home to the President and Vice President, the Provost, the Vice Provost, the Deputy Vice Provosts. The Deans of Student Life, Student Affairs, Student Concerns, Student Wishes, Student Fancies, the Vice Deans, the Dean of Deans. If we still used any of those titles."

"And all the upper floors?" J. asked. The building had had additional floors added some years back, J. would eventually learn when he read the rest of the Information Desk literature stuffed in his jacket pocket.

"Department of Community Values. See?" Carved in bold block letters in the stone arch over the main doors were some of the community's most fundamental values: BENEVOLENCE,

CHARITY, LOVINGKINDNESS. "Quick, let's catch that elevator."

They went through the doors, caught the open elevator waiting for them.

"But why," J. asked as they waited for the elevator doors to close, "am I going to see your—" He stopped, unable to think of what to call the administrator.

"Patience, grasshopper," Robert said.

"And what about the student newspaper?" J. remembered after a long moment of silence as he began pressing the elevator's "close door" button.

"That button doesn't do anything, grasshopper," Robert ignored him, putting his hand on J.'s. "Just there to give you the illusion of individual liberty."

"This is the slowest elevator I have ever experienced," J. observed moments later as they finally made their slow ascent.

"To remind you of your lack of liberty. Ah, we're here."

They walked out into a waiting area. A young woman wearing a bright yellow sari and sporting flesh tunnel earrings big enough to squeeze a thumb through lazily looked up, indicated they could take a seat on the low plush sofa along the wall, then returned to expertly manipulating her phone despite her multicolored fingernails being at least an inch and a half long.

"How does she do that?" J. whispered to Robert.

"No idea. But I think it's a 'he.' I had him in my topology class last year. Brilliant kid, despite the fashion philosophy."

"Robert," J. said again, "why am I here?"

"It's nothing, grasshopper."

"Stop calling me that! And what's nothing?"

"It's probably nothing. Just precautionary."

"What are you, the librarian now? Speaking in opaque parables?"

Robert straightened his bowtie. "Look, there was this thing in the student newspaper. It's not a big deal but Aal asked me to bring you in, just to be safe. Here, I'll show you."

But as Robert pulled out his phone the person in the sari called out in a sleepy deep voice, "Friend Aaliyah will see you now."

They were led into a roomy office distinguished by the many colorful cushions scattered on the enormous colorful Persian rug and the absence of any conventional furniture. The scent of incense filled the space. A woman in a billowy multicolored gown seated on a cushion put her hands together on her chest, palm to palm, bowed gently in greeting, and said, "As-salāmu ʿalaykum. Please, my dears, sit where you like."

"Thank you," J. took a cushion.

"Welcome to New Ghana, J.," Robert took another. "Friend J., meet friend Aaliyah, your new long-lost pal."

"Please," the Vice President said warmly to J., "You can call me Aal. And I'll kindly ask you, friend Robert, to stop referring to this office as 'New Ghana.'"

"Free speech! Viewpoint diversity!" Robert protested. "Budget cuts across the college, but the admin comrades import their office furniture from across the globe. You know how Persian rugs are supposed to have a flaw, because only the alleged Comrade in the Sky is flawless? I have it on good authority that this rug's flaw is that it is actually flawless. Comrade knows what they paid for it."

"Friend Robert enjoys his tenure," Aal said cheerfully, then turned to indicate a lanky student with a goatee seated in the corner of the room, laptop atop lap. "And please meet Shawn. He's my student shadow this week, from Undergraduate Social Support Resources. Now, may I offer you something to drink, my dear?"

"Would there be—just straight coffee?" J. asked hopefully.

Aal chortled. "Good one, friend! I can offer you pomo, of course. Or have you had the opportunity to try poco?"

"And what is poco?" J. asked hopefully again.

"I believe it's a blend of pomo and cola. It's officially served only above," she pointed upward, "but we sometimes can squirrel some away for ourselves. On occasion faculty are permitted a drop as well. When they behave." Friend Aal winked at Robert as she said this.

"They got rid of coffee on campus a couple years ago," Robert explained. "The Student Capitalists revolted against the Fair Trade policy the student government had adopted against Big Coffee, in fact they occupied these very offices specifically demanding Unfair Trade coffee. The eventual compromise was to boycott all coffee from campus. As for the poco," he added, "some people love it but all I can say is it's nasty. Drink down a bottle and you're ready to kill. I'm not sure if that's a plus or a minus. But there is one thing the grown-ups all agree on."

"And that is?" J. asked.

"We keep it out of the hands of students. Am I right, Shawn? Does Bossy Boss Bacharo let his shadowlings at the poco?"

They looked at the shadow, whose only reaction was to begin typing on his laptop.

"Perhaps, then," J. turned back to the group, "we can just— get started?"

"Of course, of course," Aal said. "So let me just begin by saying immediately that I see nothing to discipline you for, my dear."

"That's a relief," J. responded with relief, until he realized from her glance at Shawn that there was something which she could, conceivably, consider disciplining him for.

"Aal," Robert said, "he hasn't seen the *Howler* yet."

"Ah, I see. Well, then, shall we rectify that?"

The Vice President pulled over her laptop, hit a few keys, then swiveled it around so that J. could see the homepage of the newspaper. There was a large headline consisting merely of the word "THIS," followed by a colon and a web address.

"Oh, apologies," Aal said and clicked on the link, which took them to another site on which was posted an opinion piece addressed to "The Community of Nevergreen College." It began:

> We are enraged, and numb. There are dangerous forces there, right there in your home, in your heart, on your sacred ground. If you do not stamp out the hate within, then you become that hate. You must resist that hate.
>
> You must hate that hate.

And you must hate it now.

The byline was someone or something called The Resistance.

"That's odd," J. said, noticing the two angry face emojis at the bottom and thinking that *enraged* and *numb* seemed mutually exclusive. "What is the Resistance? And what does this article have to do with me?"

"Do you—" the administrator began, then scrolled down some paragraphs to the bottom of the article, "Did you have some interaction with this young woman? Some altercation, perhaps?"

On the screen was a photo of the young woman with severe eyes at the Student Clubs Expo.

"Altercation? What? No. I—met her. But why are you calling me in about this article? What does this have to do with me?"

Aal glanced over at Shawn. "Well, it isn't so much the article, I'm afraid. It's the complaint that was filed above a short while ago. The violation."

"Violation?"

"Of the Virtue Code, my dear. An Offensiveness Complaint."

"But again. What does that have to do with me."

"I am sorry for being unclear. The complaint has been filed against you."

"I don't understand."

"The Virtue Code spells out a procedure for individuals—" Robert began.

"No," J. interrupted. "I mean, what did I do?"

"I am afraid," Aal answered, "I cannot give you that information."

"I don't understand. I'm charged with something and you can't even tell me what?"

"It's confidential. To protect the plaintiffs, my dear."

"Plaintiffs? Was there—more than one?"

"I'm sorry, I cannot give you that information."

"I don't understand—Aal. Was it something I said?"

"Possibly. Not necessarily."

J. couldn't think. Who had he spoken to on campus? The

students in front of the library? That woman at the Clubs Expo, who apparently wrote the opinion piece or maybe just represented The Resistance? She had glared at him but what had he said to her? Nothing, nothing at all. He was distressed at the thought that he may have offended somebody; but even more distressed at the thought that—he hadn't.

His talk last night?

There had been no one there to hear it.

"What," he asked tentatively, "are the possible consequences of an Offensiveness Complaint?"

Aal sighed. "I don't actually know, my dear. The Virtue Code addresses complaints between students and against professors by students. Apparently we lack rules governing complaints from outside organizations against visitors. I understand that Bob has already petitioned the good people on the Virtue Committee above to work on rectifying that."

"Bob?"

"Comrade in Chief," Robert said. "The President."

"If we still used that title," Aal glanced at Shawn.

"You said outside organization," J. said, his mind racing.

Aal grimaced, glanced at Shawn. "Ah, I wasn't supposed to reveal that. An honest mistake, I assure you. I trust we can keep that amongst ourselves?" At least she hadn't revealed, she thought, that they weren't entirely certain the organization was an outside one.

"So what happens next?" J. asked, unconcerned with Aal's concern.

"Well, I hope you will stay on campus until this works itself out."

"Do I have a choice? I've been unable, so far, to figure out how to get off campus." He still hadn't heard back from Brenda and had no information about the ferry schedule. Maybe he should just head down to the dock and wait—

"Of course you have a choice, my dear. You are a free agent. You may freely accept our firm insistence that you remain on campus. We just hope you are as committed to virtue as we are here, and will choose to remain among us until the wheels of virtue have had a chance to turn."

So, what, leaving would mean he was somehow opposed to virtue?

Maybe he should call Debra.

No. The thing was absurd. He could handle it on his own. She would say.

"Fine," J. lifted his hands, in surrender.

"Wonderful, thank you," Aal said with a warm toothy smile that revealed (J. thought) a perhaps early case of periodontitis. "As there is a process that is automatically triggered whenever an OC is filed. The first step is that the offended party may present its perspective, its preferences, its wishes directly to the offending party, if they choose. And in this case, the plaintiffs have demanded you meet with their representatives. Have a conversation. I am delighted to inform you that they have selected some of our finest students to represent them in this capacity. A real testament to the quality and integrity of our community."

"They just get to demand this? Don't the grown-ups around here," J. said, unable to think of a better word, "have some say in the process?" He noticed that Shawn began typing furiously when he said this.

"We are all equal here, my dear. Everybody belongs to everybody. If that is what they want, then we want it as well."

"And that would resolve the complaint?"

"Possibly. Not necessarily. But it's a start, my dear."

"I really don't understand, Aal."

"The ways of virtue," the administrator said, flashing the V signal for virtue, "can be mysterious. But surely there is no harm in a little conversation with their representatives, is there, my dear?"

"Yes," Robert chimed in, "good things always come from a little 'conversation' with the Politburo."

"Or perhaps," Aal rebuked him, "we can all learn a little something from our students, friend Robert?"

"She's referring," Robert turned to J., "to my opposition, a few years back, to the proposal that students assume teaching responsibilities for some of the classes here. Nonsense dressed up as sense, I said, and pushed the radical line that, generally speaking, professors are better prepared to serve as professors while the students are better prepared to serve as. You know. Students. I lost. Isn't that right, Shawn?"

J. saw that the shadow's fingers were flying over his laptop keys.

"Come now, my dear," Aal said to J. "It's almost twelve. I believe the students are waiting for you upstairs."

12

ON HIS ACQUIESCENCE THEY had been taken directly upstairs one flight. In a normal place this would have put them on the fourth floor, but here, J. noticed in the elevator, the buttons for the floor above 3 were renumbered starting with "1." *Shangri-La* were the words that came to his mind when the doors opened on the waiting area, a beautiful, airy, light space with gorgeous furniture and the sounds of chirping birds being pumped in. Not just a drinking fountain but an actual fountain, with several levels, was gurgling a dark reddish liquid meant for consumption, based on the compostable cups beside it inviting you to partake.

"Welcome, friend J.," said long-haired Luiz Bacharo, Vice or Virtue Dean or not-Dean of the Department of Community Values, not greeting Robert, "to Undergraduate Social Support Resources. I am so glad you chose to come. Can I offer you some poco before we begin?"

"What? None for me?" Robert asked. "The minority of one?"

"No," Luiz said flatly. "Friend J.?"

"No, thank you," J. answered, following him down the hallway decorated, as far as he could surmise, with portraits of muppets made up as famous historical characters. The only problem was he didn't recognize any of them. Most wore colorful garb from places around the globe, robes, headdresses, interesting jewelry, one with a broad ivory nose-ring dangling from his external meatus. Wait, that one with the enormous bush of white beard and hair: familiar. Another, that dark beret with the flaming star insignia, iconic portrait, that—

"Here we are," Luiz was saying. "Room 101. The Virtue Room."

"Why 101? Aren't we on the fourth floor?" J. followed him in, following up on his unasked question about the elevator buttons.

"We renumber on the transition to the Department of Community Values," Luiz replied, directing him to a surely expensive, faux-leather chair.

"Another wonderful initiative from Big Sis Sora," Robert said.

"Actually it was mostly my idea," Luiz interjected.

"Remind me …?" J. asked.

"Head honcho here," Robert pointed upward. "Or honcha, I suppose. Office on top floor of the tower. With the additional stories they say she now has a 360-degree view of the entire campus."

"Mine, soon," Luiz whispered accidentally, then looked around to see if anyone had heard him.

"Professor Merritt," said a familiar voice whose use of that archaic title indicated its scorn, "will you please refrain from insulting this institution for thirty seconds? Bob requested that we get started as soon as possible."

It was friend Peace, whose mood was clearly of anything but.

"Ah, our esteemed mistress of conflict," Robert answered, "who before depriving our community of the inalienable right to meat deprived us of the inalienable right to individual privacy. It was she who, in the name of promoting peace, placed cameras and microphones in the stones." He turned to J. "She's probably listening to our conversation right now."

"Robert, I can hear you directly," Peace growled. "I'm sitting right here."

"See? Oh hey, what's he doing here?"

J. turned to look at the room. Bright, decorated in what J. thought was a Middle Eastern style. Colorful mosaics adorning the columns, the two candle-shaped niches in one wall, even the faux-fireplace behind him. Exotic lanterns hung from the ceiling, and looping calligraphy, phrases in Arabic script perhaps, wound around the perimeter above and at spots in the side paneling. They had seated J. at the head of the room, with friend

Luiz to his left and friend Peace to his right. To Luiz's left was his student shadow, Harpya, laptop open and ready. There was no seat for Robert, who was momentarily to be thanked for escorting J. to the room then asked to leave. On the side of the room, where Robert had been pointing, silently sat Dr. Taslitz M. Fester in his wheelchair.

"He is here," Luiz calmed himself by twirling his hair, "to hear the students."

"So that the students may be heard," Peace added.

"Speaking of …?" J. asked.

"Behind there." Peace pointed at the three large Shoji screens partitioning the room. "To protect the students, when they are being heard."

"Shall we begin?" Luiz held up the V signal to indicate the quest for virtue. "Friend J., would you like to begin with a statement? A confession, perhaps?"

"A confession?" J. answered, confused, aware that the student shadow had begun typing. "I'm not entirely sure—"

"Could you have him speak up?" a disembodied female voice said from behind the screens. "We need better sound levels." There was scuffling on the other side of the screen; recording devices being set up.

"Friend?" Peace asked.

"Testing one two three," J. obliged, loudly.

"Better," another perhaps male voice interrupted.

"Shall we begin?" Luiz asked again.

"The Resistance has directed me," a perhaps female voice immediately started, possibly identical to the first one, but angrier, "to report that there are just, like, so many problems on this campus. Just to start with, like, this morning …"

J.'s mind wandered as the young person launched into an account of the so many problems on this campus. He checked back in periodically, noting, after a while, that the problems didn't seem to have anything to do with him. The difficulties transgendered students had with campus bathrooms, for example.

Shorter science students had trouble seeing the whiteboards in the classrooms in Hexant 3, and in any case what was the racial significance of blackboards being replaced by whiteboards in so many classrooms? There should also be trigger warnings on syllabi when a course required reading. Or wait, perhaps that was a different student speaking. It was hard to determine how many students there were. At least several but they were hard to distinguish, female, male. Hadn't he always gotten along perfectly fine with females? And males? At some point he realized the students were bickering among themselves. Someone was opposed to the slogan "Keep It Crazy" because it was offensive to the crazy. Because of free speech someone else opposed painting over the Lodge 3 mural, after the repainting (because of free speech) of the controversial original mural was vandalized (because of free speech). There was an argument over just what position the Resistance actually took concerning the campus Big Chief statue—recently torn down because it was a form of dehumanizing cultural appropriation but then rebuilt as an exact replica in respect and appreciation of native culture—all of which was now feeding into the Halloween controversy that was on the verge of exploding all over the Hex—

There was a long, deep, soul-searing moan.

The other side of the Shoji screens fell silent, and all eyes on this side turned to Dr. Fester, who had released the sound.

"Under control!" Peace reached over to pick up the book that had slipped out of Dr. Fester's hand. As she returned it to his lap J. could see its title: *Humour and Pus*, by one Dr. Taslitz M. Fester, the man's very last book containing his very last words.

All in all the fifty-five minutes went extremely quickly, J. thought when it was over, even with the five-minute break for one of the students to find her charger and plug in her phone.

13

"How DID IT GO, my dear?" friend Aaliyah asked as they debriefed in her office. Peace had had to depart quickly, the theater folks requiring an emergency consult on their staging of *An Emergency*. Luiz had escorted J. back down to the administration level, and now sat on one of the cushions feeling that sweet aggressive energy from the masterful way he was handling the current situation or from the poco he was sipping, or both.

"You can appeal the sentence," Robert interrupted from another cushion. "If they demanded you be burned, we can argue for drowning instead."

"Robert, please," Aaliyah said.

"If you are to be drawn and quartered, I know a kick-ass lawyer," Robert continued. "Get that knocked down to halving, lickety-split."

"Robert, *please*," Aaliyah repeated.

"Did they demand you wear the scarlet 'H' on your jacket? That's a common—"

"Cool your jets, friend Robert," Luiz interrupted. "There was no sentencing. In fact I'd say he handled himself very well."

"But I didn't say a word," J. said.

"That's what I mean."

J. felt some tension in his stomach as he turned back to Aaliyah. "So, what—can we say—is the Offensiveness Complaint resolved?"

"Oh, definitely not," Aaliyah glanced at Shawn and Harpya, both busy typing on their cushions.

"What?"

"Well the students will have to confer with the Resistance of course, and gauge the movement's feelings. Then I will have to confer with the students, to gauge *their* feelings about those feelings. Then confer with Bob, and gauge Bob's feelings. Then I'll gauge my own feelings, and make a recommendation."

"To whom?" J. asked.

"To myself, probably. As I mentioned, my dear, the rules here aren't very clear. But in the meanwhile, might I advise that you draft a statement, for the *Howler*? I think that would go a long way toward appeasing the hurt."

"A statement?"

"A confession, specifically."

"Again with a confession. But what for?"

"The Resistance thought it would be a good idea."

"I mean what should I confess to? Specifically?"

"This isn't that difficult," Luiz jumped in, nodding at Harpya. "How about some of your views? Or positions?"

"On what?"

"You must have some controversial opinions."

J. felt that tension again in his stomach. As Debra liked to put it, the most controversial opinion he had ever expressed was that one time he insisted to her he *was* capable of making up his own mind about something, immediately before he solicited her advice on that very decision.

"I don't," he said softly.

"Well, then, your language."

"My language?"

"The way you *expressed* your opinions."

"Which opinions?"

"It doesn't matter. It's all about the language."

"What language? I really don't understand, Luiz."

Aaliyah resumed the lead. "It doesn't really matter, my dear. The Resistance feels like a confession. I think it's necessary to give them one. Maybe that could, you know. Help us resolve the offensiveness incident. The complaint. So we could let you go."

"Let me go? What does that—"

"Aal is right," Luiz interrupted as his heart accelerated a notch and his hair grew in a spurt. "We must resolve this matter as soon as possible. I want to see that beautiful white smoke billowing into our gorgeous blue fall sky by the end of business today."

"I literally have no idea what any of you are talking about," J. said in exasperation.

"Just imagine working here," Robert chimed in. "But I can tell you that the friendly illuminati in the values department like to alert the public when virtue has been achieved. Big Sis Sora has a smokestack coming out of her office."

"It was my idea," Luiz inserted, glancing at Harpya.

"Take ten minutes right now," friend Aaliyah said suddenly quite firmly, "and save us all some headache. You can use my computer." She slid her laptop along the floor toward him. "Just come out and get me when you're done. I'll take a quick look before passing it on. I understand from Corrie that The Resistance would like it posted by three." She glanced at Shawn, then at Luiz, who nodded in affirmation.

"Corrie?" J. asked, yielding.

"Commando-in-Chief of the student newspaper," Robert said. "Local liaison to the global Resistance movement, apparently."

"Tall girl, severe eyes?" J. felt nauseous.

"And cold-stone heart."

"Friend Robert," Luiz reminded him sternly as he stood to leave the room with Aaliyah, "you know the Virtue Code forbids saying negative things about students."

"Actually I meant it," Robert said after they'd left the room, "as a compliment."

14

Free speech is something we all support. But does that mean free speech must always be allowed? No. Not when your free speech hurts people. Not when it offends a community. Especially a community that has Community Values. A community that rejects hate. That hates nothing but hate itself. That hates *hate*.

"That was fast," J. said, stunned.

Robert scratched his beard. "The wonders of modern technology."

Fast, indeed. After submitting the draft of his confession to Aaliyah, J. and Robert had headed out for lunch. Back out in the Hex they went around the Maze by going through Hexant 6, past the Adorno building, and Hexant 5. The latter was defined by a striking glass Pacman, home, Robert said, to a recently renovated state of the art gym; this despite the budget cuts and the fact that the school had abolished competitive sports some years back. Passing behind Lodge 5 they found the barbecue stand set up by the Carnivores Club, as a political statement, outside the first dining hall to go vegan, the one in the Beatrice Nah Center for the Unapplied Sciences in Hexant 3. Business had improved sharply with the passing of the vegan ordinance, but the future obviously was unclear.

"Ah, look," Robert said as they approached The Spit, pointing to one of the tables. "Professor Ntombizanele Thatch. History of Female Yadda-Yadda. But she's all right. A possible ally for you. Thatch! May we join you?"

"Can I stop you, darling?" Thatch replied with an unusual

accent, standing up a full six foot ten and dwarfing J.'s hand in hers after Robert made the introduction.

"Would be fun if you tried!" Robert and J. placed their trays on the table and took their seats. "Thatch was a former basketball star, if you haven't already guessed."

"My passport out of South Africa," Thatch added, thus also explaining the accent.

"So get this," Robert began the story of the growing campus crisis. It was when he checked the *Howler*'s website to show Thatch J.'s now public confession that they saw the new story placed directly beneath it, again consisting solely of the word "This" followed by a colon and a link to the Resistance website. There they saw the new article, which had so far earned several hearts and one angry face with smoking ears emoji.

"Who are Cerise and Viresce?" J. asked quietly, noting that this piece had names in the byline.

"*Noms de guerre* of the movement's leaders, maybe?" Robert suggested.

"Hates hate," Thatch applied a heap of spicy mustard to her sausage. "Pretty catchy."

"I know, right?" Robert concurred. "J. here's got this roost in a ruckus."

"You?" Thatch turned to J., examined him. "You're the fellow they're all worked up about?"

"Apparently."

"Hm. Well I fail to see what the ruckus is about, darling. After all, what you said at your lecture was perfectly true."

"But you can't know what I said. No one was there."

"Of course. But if the roost is in a ruckus about it, it must have been true."

"Thatch," Robert explained, "likes ruffling the occasional feather. She was openly attracted to women before it was cool to be a lesbian. Then when everyone was a lesbian she declared herself cured. Now *that* was a ruckus! And who was the last Black South African you met who actually championed Apartheid?"

"Blanks," J. admitted.

"Not to mention the great critic of toxic femininity, the pioneer of post-feminism feminism. Women's interests, turns out, are best served by the suppression of women's interests. Thatch even proved this mathematically in her truly roost-ruckusing book, *Wenches, Witches, and Whores: A Woman's Proper Place*."

"With your help with the mathematics, darling Robert," Thatch acknowledged, her dark skin blushing.

"In fact, now that I think of it," Robert clapped J. on the back, "you and Thatch have a lot in common. That stuff with paintings, medicine. J. here writes about flaying, I believe he said. Dr. Tulp, was it, if I'm not mistaken?"

"Really, darling," Thatch turned to J. "Then you must know the nineteenth-century boxwood and ivory figurine of—"

"*Dr. Nicolaes Tulp Giving an Anatomical Lecture*," J. completed the sentence, "I do. After the Anatomy Act put an end to grave robbing, artist unknown, and substituting—"

"—a female corpse for Rembrandt's executed criminal," Thatch returned the favor, "Smashing, darling! And so you must *also* know of Hasselhorst's 1864—"

"*Dissection of a Young, Beautiful Woman in Order to Determine the*—"

"*Ideal Female Proportions*," Thatch smiled. "I wrote my first Ph.D. on those works. Which turned into my second book, on the history of venereal disease in women."

"Now *that* made for some bedtime reading," Robert beamed. "*M'Lady's Humours and Pus*. Thus marking the beginning, for those taking notes, of your—"

"—long intellectual love affair with the female anus, yes," Thatch said with a long satisfied sigh.

There was a moment of silence as this point sunk in.

"Yikes!" Robert suddenly exclaimed, having resumed skimming his phone, "Have a look at this. Stroll down to the comments."

J. looked again at the article on the Resistance website, then the fourteen comments already posted on it.

"What—is happening?" he said, not knowing what else to say.

"They're just kids," Thatch said gently.

"They're so hostile."

"You're not kidding," Robert agreed. "Look at this emoji." He pointed at the two oversized hands with the extended middle fingers.

"Are they even students from here?" J. asked. "They just identify as generic 'Students.' And they seem like fake names. 'Peggy-O'? 'Scaramouche'? 'Mercy Mercy Mr. Percy'?"

"*Noms de guerre?*" Robert speculated again. "Or who knows? These days anything is a name."

"From here or not, I wouldn't worry, darling," Thatch continued to console. "It's not really about you, after all. You're just the excuse. The trigger. They're blowing off steam."

"But they—why are they so hostile toward *me?*"

"If we understood how their minds work," Robert offered, "I'm sure we'd be far more effective teachers."

"Hey! Is one even allowed to do that?" J. said with urgency as he refreshed Robert's screen. "As an administrator?"

"What?"

A fifteenth comment had just been posted.

> A community must inoculate itself against germs of hate.
> The one thing we must hate is hate itself. We must hate *hate.*

It was signed, "Administrator."

"'Hate hate,'" Robert observed, nodding. "That *is* pretty catchy."

"He or she is just doing their job, darling," Thatch said. "You know they have so many administrators now they have to keep themselves busy."

"I want to leave now," J. said. "I'll just go down to the dock and wait for—"

As he said that Thatch's phone rang. She answered and handed it over to J., who handed Robert's phone back to Robert without even wondering how the Vice President had known to call him on Thatch's phone.

"Ah, I'm glad to reach you, my dear," friend Aaliyah said, a bit out of breath as she was walking while she talked. "How fare you?"

"Frankly, I've been better."

"I imagine. I am really terribly sorry about those online comments. They are not very generous. I do not often say this, but you know, they are just kids."

"I really don't understand. I confessed."

"That was a bad move, apparently."

"But you told me to."

"I thought it would appease them. How could I know they would take it as an affirmation of your guilt?"

"Isn't that your job? To know things like this?" J. was surprised to hear the rising anger in his voice.

"My dear," Aal paused to catch her breath, "we all have much to learn. We must let the students guide us in this matter."

"Look," J. said, speaking more quickly. "I'm a very nice person. The only one who ever gets angry at me is my wife, who yells at me because I am generally nice even to people who are mean to me. I really could do without a dozen people writing nasty comments about me."

"It is closer to two dozen, my dear."

"What?"

"When did you last check?"

"Three minutes ago."

"Check again."

J. beckoned to Robert, who refreshed the screen. "Twenty-one comments on this editorial now. At least two," J. added, feeling sick, "identify themselves as faculty. Aren't they supposed to be—you know—the grown-ups around here?"

"They just say generically they are 'Faculty,' my dear, and I don't recognize the names. They may not even be from here. And in any case, my dear, there are over 1,100 students at this school, and almost 100 faculty. Twenty-one comments aren't significant."

"Twenty-nine comments," J. corrected her, the screen refreshed again, "three by 'Faculty.' Some three dozen hearts, smiley faces, middle fingers. One weepy face."

"It is not really about you."

"Most of the comments use my name. Several threaten me, by name."

"I promise you do not need to worry. Even if they are from here—and I admit nothing—they do not even know what you look like, my dear. You'll mix in with the tourists."

The tourists, J. thought. He had seen several others on their walk through the Hex. They were walking around with cameras taking selfies with the crazy students at the asylum and snapping piles of pig shit. But he did not look anything like a tourist.

His fingers tightened on the phone when he remembered that that girl—Corrie—had taken a photo of him.

"But listen, my dear," the Vice President continued. "The newspaper is not the reason I am calling."

"What, then?"

Her voice became quieter. "There's a second Offensiveness Complaint against you. I am sorry."

"I don't understand. For what?"

"For your confession."

"My confession?"

"The Resistance didn't think it was sincere. They found it hurtful. Intolerant of the hurt they were feeling."

J. didn't say anything.

"You will come back to my office later this afternoon. Or this evening. I shall have spoken with Bob by then, and then you and I shall talk it all through. After the gathering. We shall figure out what to do. Ah, hold on." There was a shuffling and rustling on the other end. J. could hear the Vice President muttering something.

"What was that?" he asked.

"My apologies. Just arrived back at my building and had to remove the tape."

"The tape?"

"Across the front door. Holding up the—banner."

"Banner?"

"I am sure it is nothing, my dear."

"It obviously is something, otherwise you wouldn't be so uncomfortable."

"It says, 'Hate *Hate*,'" Aal said softly. "It is rather catchy actually. They're calling for an official Two Minutes of Hate-Hate later this afternoon. Truth be told, I am actually so darn proud of this community."

J. barely heard the administrator hang up. Robert's refreshed screen now showed forty-one comments, five by faculty members. Dozens of emojis now, weepy faces, fuming faces, shocked faces, one "The Scream," a dancing Hitler gif.

A comment from someone explicitly identifying himself as being off campus.

"Ignore all that, darling, it will only upset you," Thatch said compassionately. "Talk to me instead. What do you do, sir, when you're not inciting riots? That has you writing tomes about our darling Dr. Tulp?"

Not a philosopher, J. thought. "Doctor."

"Ah, you're useful."

"I try to be."

"That's healthy. A great deal healthier than the academentia you find around here, I would say."

Academentia, J. thought, admiring the term, must remember to tell Debra.

"Check this out, people," Robert had refreshed his phone again. "I think the tide may be turning."

There was another article on the Resistance site called "In Defense of Virtue," in which Cerise and Viresce demanded that last night's speaker be found and detained, brought up on a fair trial before the Virtue Code Court, then sentenced to public shaming followed by expulsion from campus.

"I thought you said the tide was turning," J. said unhappily.

"I didn't say for the better."

"It's incoherent, really," Thatch noted. "It both demands a fair trial and prejudges the outcome. It demands the expulsion of someone who is only visiting campus in the first place. Must be some of your students, Robert."

Robert chortled. "True enough, if they are from this god-forsaken campus. But we can't all be blessed with an Elijah, Thatch, now can we?"

"My darling prize student," Thatch sighed. "The student teaching whom almost compensates for dealing with all the—" she hesitated, "the rest. Elijah is a dream."

"How is the first op-ed doing?" J. asked, miserable.

"Ooh," Robert groaned.

"Bad?"

"Fifty-four comments. A lot explicitly from off-campus now. Oh."

"What?"

"The 'Hate *Hate*' meme is really flying. There are a couple from Europe. One from Asia. The Middle East. Ouch! That is one frightening emoji someone just invented. I wouldn't check your email if I were you. It's now a hashtag."

That, fortunately, wasn't much of a concern for J., who had never really seen the need for email. On that rare occasion he used it, it was usually to send videos of adorable baby animals to his wife. Who had repeatedly requested he cease anyway.

"It really isn't about you, my darling," Thatch said again. "It is the idea of you. Of what you represent. That sort of thing."

"And what do I represent?" J. asked glumly.

"Everything they dislike. The powers that be," Thatch paused. "The new boss, same as the old boss. At root they feel bad they missed the '60s. They've heard about it, they want to be an activist about something. They want to shut down the campus. For something. For anything."

"But why me? Why am I the 'new boss'?"

"Why not you? You were there. Right time, right place. Or

whatever. You know, when I was reading for my undergraduate degree we got our bloomers in a twist about the toilet tissue. You know, in every building, in the dorms. They had these little slips of paper, absurdly thin. They tore in your hands. One weekend we marched on the Master's house in the middle of the night, ejected him and his family, and defecated without flushing all night long in all of his toilets. We refused to leave until they agreed to replace the toilet tissue."

"And?"

"We all got arrested. It was superb."

"And the toilet paper?"

"From next semester onwards, we had two-ply. It was very empowering, my darling."

"I'm leaving," J. stood up. "I'll just head down to the ferry and wait."

Robert grimaced. "They're only like twice a day. Next one's not until evening I believe. Listen, I have my seminar in a few minutes but—"

Just then loud noises could be heard coming out of the building a short distance away. Crowd noises, some clapping, a megaphone.

"Ah," Thatch looked at her own phone. "I just got an alert. Looks like they have got a Teach-In starting at three, before the gathering. Might be interesting to go have a look?"

"But," J. protested, "I'm not exactly comfortable showing my face in there."

"You're forgetting something, darling friend J."

"What?"

"None of them was at your talk last night."

"So?"

"You have no web presence, you say. You're not on social media. You have literally never been in the news, you say."

"So?"

Thatch clucked. "They don't know what you look like."

PART III

SOMETHING IS ROTTEN
ON THIS CAMPUS

15

LAUREN WAS HAVING TROUBLE fitting in.

She didn't like working at The Spit. It was smelly and greasy and she wasn't sure it was sanitary. And these kids who ran it weren't her type, or maybe she wasn't their type. But this was the best-paying job left by the time she finally committed to Nevergreen, unlike almost everyone else here who seemed to have this place as their first choice. She was just feeling relieved that her shift was ending when the alert came about the Teach-In. She wasn't sure what this was. Weren't colleges already about teaching, so how was this supposed to be different from normal? Nor was she eager to return to the Intersections Lounge after that awkward morning wandering booth to booth and not feeling that any of the student clubs was for her. She briefly thought maybe the Marshmallow Club, but then the hostility from the adjacent Anti-Marshmallow Club was daunting. She wished she could shower. She smelled like sausage, she thought. She wished she could go back to the lodge and shower and put her favorite sweatshirt back on, the loosely fitting yellow hoodie with her high school logo, but there wasn't time. She came to college to learn, she figured, and whatever a Teach-In was, it was presumably something where something was to be learned.

As she entered the lounge, pushing through the many students entering with her, she felt as if all eyes were on her, as if everybody knew she had no idea what this was about, what she was supposed to do. She felt the same way about her virginity, which she was sure was also visibly obvious to everyone and about which she was equally ashamed. In both instances her instinct was to go hole up in her room and stay out of public with her shame. But that was only an incomplete fix, as her roommate Baara was already big into political activism and made her feel like an idiot and her other roommate Keziah was into something called polymorphous perversity she had learned about in her class on male sexuality, which as far as Lauren could tell meant she wanted sex not merely any time but with nearly any *thing*. Suffice to say that Lauren was not comfortable sharing even toothpaste with her roommate, much less a bedroom.

Well what she did know was that whatever was happening here today was important. Some serious violation of community values had occurred, hate had visited her campus, her home away from home, and it was essential, crucial—the student facilitators of her 4:00 PM class had said in their text alert, cancelling the class and mandating attendance at the Teach-In—that she understand the many ramifications of this.

The lounge had been transformed since this morning's Expo. Shoji screens now divided the large space into four smaller spaces. According to the flyer the student captains were handing out, there were to be four parallel panel discussions, each lasting twenty minutes, then repeated three times after short breaks so that each student could participate in all four during the two-hour event. The session would end with the a cappella group, Universal Harmony, leading everyone in Nevergreen's soon-to-be-official solidarity hymn: *O Best Possible World Where Virtuous Virtue Reigns*. Break-out spaces were of course available should students need some respite from hearing about all the hate. The "Safe and Sound" rooms were softly lit, carpeted, stocked with milk, cookies, and stuffed animals, with soothing nature sounds playing: birds tweeting, surf licking the shore, moving mournful whale calls. This was Lauren's favorite thing about Nevergreen, the somasound, the meditative background music pumped through the speakers throughout campus. Calm sounds, calm body, the mind prepared for learning.

She hesitated on entering, overwhelmed by the space, the people jostling her as they filed in. Maybe she should just begin in a Safe and Sound room, maybe just stay there. She sniffed and realized, with relief, that there was a scent of pomo in the air, and immediately felt better. Initially she found the stuff repulsive, but now some nine weeks into the semester she was acquiring the taste. In fact, she thought, the soft scent of it was almost—

Sublime. That was a word, she thought.

"Lauren!" a voice called to her. Her roommate Keziah approached. "What are you starting with?"

"I—don't know. You?"

"Definitely the stuffed animals," Keziah was clearly in a hurry to get started.

Well, so much for the stuffed animals, Lauren thought. She looked back at her flyer. There were so many possibilities: "How Hate Hurts," "How Hate Is Violence," "Free Speech and Hate Speech," "Hate Speech and Hate Silence." As she read these she felt her breathing quicken, her temperature rise, feeling the outrage that hate, no, *Hate*, had happened on her own campus, her home, her—cocoon. Here! She realized she felt violated, and angry, not just at the Hate here but at the world for allowing Hate to exist in the first place, for fostering it, spreading it. The problem was so large. And if it couldn't be stamped out here, at Nevergreen, then how could they ever stamp it out in the world at large? But the first step was learning about it, and she now knew she had come to the right place. She was grateful to the student facilitators who would lead these sessions, which affirmed, she thought, taking a long, deep, satisfying breath, that she had come to the right school after all.

We must hate *hate*, she was thinking as she took her seat in the section that would teach her "How Hate Hurts." She was so absorbed in learning how hate germs corrupt a community from within that she didn't notice the man standing at the rear of the section, with a small group of Japanese tourists, listening with a scowl on his face. She was then so absorbed learning about the many ways that hate hurts—explicit and implicit, short term and long term, intellectually and emotionally, mind and body— that she did not notice when the man walked off abruptly to the adjacent section on "How Hate Is Violence," which spared her the feeling of violence she may have had at seeing someone fail to value a value she so valued. Some forty-five minutes later she was also so absorbed in learning that silence in the presence of hate was itself a form of Hate Speech that she did not notice the other growing activity going on behind her.

She did notice, however, when the harsh blast of sound violently penetrated the calm cawing of distant seagulls being pumped into the room.

16

"LISTEN UP, BOYS AND girls!" came the voice over the hijacked P.A. system. "Nobody move! Resist the Resistance! This is a Teach-Out!"

"What the heck—?" Lauren exclaimed to the student next to her, her ears—still ringing from the vuvuzela blast preceding the P.A. blast—even further wounded by the gender binariness they had just suffered.

"I don't know, but bam ba lam, dude! It is *fantabulous*," said the student, whose royal crimson King Crimson t-shirt was almost as long overdue for a wash as he himself was. "Check out the gear! Who are those spectaculous people?"

Several students had infiltrated the lounge whose goals clearly were not aligned with those of the Teach-In. They were wearing matching Confederate Civil War uniforms with faux musketoons attached to their belts, their faces masked. Neither Lauren nor second-year student Nature Boy—for that was his trail name, and he was always on the trail—were competent to identify these as Confederate uniforms, much less as "musketoons." In fact neither were the students wearing them, who did so only because their ringleader had told them to.

But Lauren didn't hear what Nature Boy said, having already clamped her hands over her ears as an earlier speaker had instructed them to do in emergencies like this. "Hear no evil! Hear no evil!" she chanted repeatedly.

"Open your eyes! Close your mouth! Free your minds!" the voice on the P.A. continued. "Take a pamphlet! Take a mask!"

Nature Boy saw that the provocateurs were distributing both literature and face masks, the former under the false belief that better ideas would screen out the ones being disseminated in the Teach-In and the latter under the false belief that the masks would screen out the pomo in the air. Nature Boy was interested in neither, as reading wasn't his thing and drugs, of any form, were. Since Lauren was still frantically chanting "Hear no evil!" he turned instead to the student sitting on Lauren's other side.

"Awesome shirt, dude," he said first, admiring the logo: FUR-THER. HIGHER. FASTER. MORE. He then pointed to the young man in the corner of the lounge who had commandeered the microphone. "But what is up with that dude? And what is that phenomular rig he is rocking?"

Phineas, who prided himself on so far having a perfect attendance record in his classes this semester (namely 0%), answered, "It's the 'Colonel of Truth,' man. He always pulls outrageous shit like this."

"Like what, dude?"

"Like pushing for pomo to be banned from campus, for one."

"Fuck no way!"

"And like last year, when the student council approved the two new safe spaces. He tried to push for some unsafe spaces."

"Seriously?"

"I shit you not, man. He, like, wanted a room with broken glass on the floor. Another where you would like stick your face in a cage right up to a rabid rat. The rumor is that when they blocked his legislation he built one himself anyway. Some girl claims he tied her up and forced her to listen to speeches by Republicans."

"That is seriously awesome, dude. But, like, wouldn't that be a violation of the Virtue Code?"

"It totally is, man. But she like cracked up and left campus before filing charges. The rumor is that she's now in like a *real* asylum. Anyhow, whatever you do, do not pick up his bullshit pamphlet. And definitely do NOT go listen to him."

"Why not?"

"The other rumor is that he is really persuasive. Safer not to risk it."

"Hate hate. Bam ba lam."

"Exactly."

"But dude, what's the deal with the stupendelicious rig?"

But Phineas had become distracted. With Lauren's hands still raised to her ears her breasts were raised, beneath her shirt, to Phineas's attention, and these combined with her obvious virginity were proving irresistible. Nature Boy proved more formidable in resisting her charms, possibly because of the many Xanax pills he had swallowed on the way over here. In any case his question already seemed moot; after a minor skirmish the Virtue Patrol had removed the Colonel of Truth and his lackeys from the room and Nature Boy was fully back on the trail.

So firmly on the trail was he that he barely reacted either when, as he was busy getting his space together in preparation for the a cappella show, he picked up the pamphlet from the floor and read the title—"On the Superior Virtue of the Oppressed"— or when he flipped it over and read some slogans by the Colonel himself. "Progress is good," it proclaimed, "But all progress is generated by hate," so one should "love hate," foster "love-hate relationships." Somewhere far away he felt like maybe some interesting point was being made; but then he took a deep breath and reflected that figuring out that point would be such dreadaciously hard work and he didn't go to college to work so damn hard and bam ba lam, this was clearly hate speech, and hadn't the panelists just been explaining that genuine support for free speech required suppressing all counter speech? He took another deep satisfying breath, dropped the pamphlet in the nearby recycling bin, and then, his space all together now, headed into the show.

17

As for the aforementioned "rig," it was in fact a knock-off Confederate uniform. The Colonel himself was aware neither that it was a knock-off nor that it was a Confederate uniform, as he had clicked on the first old-looking military uniform both within his price range and available for next-day shipping and hadn't bothered reading the description. He was just glad at last to have a uniform worthy of a Colonel, particularly a Colonel of Truth, and even more glad that Amazon had informed him that "frequently bought together" with this uniform was the long faux musketoon he had managed to attach to his belt. Finally, he was simply thrilled that everything had arrived in time.

Best of all, it was already pissing people off, starting with Harpy here.

"How ... dare ... you," the little witch stammered, stuttered, hissed, confronting him outside in the Hex after he'd been thrown out of the Teach-In by the appointed muscle, "make me ... all of us ... so uncomfortable! I'm going to ... inform ... the Resistance!"

"Discomfort is the new comfort," the Colonel answered calmly, his mask removed. "Resisting the Resistance, the new Resistance. Am I right, ladies?"

The Colonel turned to his three lackeys behind him, who were wearing the matching privates uniforms he had made them pay for and who chortled, on cue, "The new Resistance!"

"Such ... flouting ... of the rules. Of our values!" Harpy shrieked, glancing at the whole crew but then glaring back at the Colonel. "Shame, shame on you! You smug piece of … *shit!*"

"Flouting is the new compliance," the Colonel answered. "Shame, the new pride. Truth, the new lie. Worthless, the new values. Am I right, ladies?"

Harpy did not wait for the chortles. "That's it, you arrogant piece of … *shit!* I'm pressing this. I'm going to. Don't test me!" She had her finger crooked over one of the Emergency buttons placed roughly every fifty yards on the campus.

"Go ahead," the Colonel marveled at his own calmness. "I don't even think they're hooked up to anything. The Elders just put them there to sedate the ignoranuses. Or should I say 'ignorani'?"

"Ignorani!" chortled the lackeys, the loudest being the Colonel's chief lackey, who liked to think of himself as the Lieutenant of Truth even after the Colonel explained that that really didn't work with the pun.

"Don't test me, you racist, rule-flouting … scum!" Harpy shrieked. Behind her, other harpies had collected, shrieking, along with an increasing crowd of spectators. The Colonel's Teach-Out had not succeeded in taking over the Teach-In, but it had drawn some people out of the lounge and into the Hex. Many students had their phones out, filming the spectacle. Two were already live-streaming onto the internet, closely monitoring their likes.

"Do it, do it, do it," the Colonel's lackeys began chanting, a chorus promptly taken up by some of the spectators.

A fanfare of trumpets and a burst into flight of hundreds of swallows interrupted the proceedings, or at least so it seemed to the Colonel when the crowds parted to allow passage to none other than the Queen Bee herself.

"What's all this, then?" Dean of Community Values Sora Rava said in her authentic British accent as she entered the space between the opposing parties. She had just been floating through the lounge absolutely bursting with pride at what her subjects were accomplishing when word reached her of the conflict brewing outside. "Harpya?" she said, surprised to see that her recent student shadow was in the middle of it.

"Friend Sora," Harpy (for so she was known to her friends and enemies alike) complained, "This ... this ... confederacy of dunces here. Especially the one in charge, this ... Alfred E. Neuman here. Just look. Look what he's wearing."

"That's Colonel Dunce to you, *harpy*," the Colonel said brusquely, always irritated when people used his given name. "And Jeebus, it's just a piece of clothing. Some fabric, some buttons, that's all."

"Clothing," muttered his lackeys behind him.

"It violates the Virtue Code!" one of Harpy's harpies behind her shouted.

"I am happy to take it off," the Colonel said. "But I should warn you that I am buck naked underneath. In all my mansome glory." He began to remove his shirt—

"Now, now, friends," Sora interrupted. "Let us stop our shouting. When we are civil with one another we can more easily resolve our differences." As she said this she made the V signal, to remind them all of virtue.

"It's not just a piece of clothing," Harpy shouted, "it's a racist piece of shit clothing, worn by a racist piece of shit! If you allow this then every piece of shit on this campus—"

"Pieces of shit!" the harpies shouted.

"Doesn't cursing also violate the Virtue Code?" the Colonel interrupted.

"Cursing pieces of shit!" the lackeys shouted.

"Please, dear friends," Sora waved her V signal more forcefully, "civility."

"Fuck civility!" Harpy shouted incivilly.

"Civility is a tool of oppression!" someone on Harpy's side in the crowd shouted.

"It's how the Elders keep us down!" the Lieutenant of Truth shouted, immediately confused by the fact that he was apparently agreeing with someone on the other side.

"Be all that as it may," friend Sora's voice elevated, "it is my commission, in my capacity as Dean of Community Values— if we still used that title—to promote civility, to create a civil space, on this campus."

"That is bullshit," Harpy said frighteningly calmly.

"Pardon? But it is my job—"

"Be quiet!" Harpy shrieked. "That is *not* your job!"

"Harpya?" friend Sora said softly, surprised both by this remark and by seeing her shadow—who had been with her for a month before rotating last week back to friend Luiz, and who had always seemed quite level-headed, and rational—acting this way against her. Could this aggressive behavior have something to do with Luiz? Sora felt terrible for wondering this, but lately, Luiz, well, especially with that, that outright *insubordination* this morning, overriding Sora's instructions about how to arrange the booths at the Student Clubs Expo, it was almost as if friend Luiz were not so friendly, and was deliberately aiming to, what, produce *unrest*—

"Your job," Harpy shouted, turning her more attractive left profile toward the students filming close-ups, "is to create a place of comfort for the students who live here! A place for us to feel at home here! At *home*! You have not done that!" She turned her head upward and looked directly into the nearest cameras. "Do you understand that?"

The Colonel thought this would be a good time to interject, "Homelessness is the new at-home."

"Shut up!" several harpies shouted simultaneously.

"Harpya," Sora was wondering whether Luiz's student shadow program was in fact designed specifically to spread Luiz's own influence in the system. "I do understand. I just disagree."

Harpy exploded. "Then why the fuck did you accept the position? Who the fuck hired you?" Here she was momentarily forgetting that she herself had chaired the student search committee that offered Sora the job four years earlier. "You should step down. Your job is not about creating a 'civil space'! It is *not*! It is about creating a home. Do you *not* understand that?!"

Sora resisted the thought about Luiz lately taking credit for Sora's own initiatives so she could resist the urge to remind little Harpya here that she, Sora, was possessed of masters and doctoral degrees in Diversity and Inclusion Theory and Practice, had turned down professorships from Oxford and Harvard to accept the Nevergreen values position because she was so attracted to the school's radically forward philosophy and relished the challenge of rebuilding the institution after The Episode, and she really didn't appreciate being lectured about "not understanding" by an undergraduate who was more than four years into, without completing, her major in coloring.

"Harpya," Sora said instead with dignity, "I am on your side here. I share your values."

"Our values?! Shut up! First you allow that, that *hate* to happen on campus, last night. And now! By not immediately expelling—" Harpy paused to think of a slur to fling at the Colonel—"that not-an-idiot-savant-but-just-plain-idiot, you are not dealing with the problem. You *are* the problem. You, with your poco-privilege! You should not sleep at night. You are *disgusting*."

"Friends, friends," Sora said quietly, her face darkening, trying to hold it together. The "poco-privilege" remark was clearly Luiz's doing, she was now sure. Sora had been pushing to democratize the poco almost since arriving, feeling the budget situation unfairly favored the values friends, but Luiz always pushed back. "We must truly value our values," Luiz always said in that sloganistic fashion of his, "and we best do that by valuing only our lead values friends with poco." But just last week that button-pushing Prof. Bowtie told her that Luiz had been telling people the opposite, that since everyone works for everyone then everyone should have poco, and that everyone *would* have poco if it weren't for friend Sora's elitist opposition ... He was probably even secretly dispensing poco to his favored students ... Luiz Bacharo was behind this, all of this, that son-of-a ...

The Colonel was enjoying himself immensely, slur notwithstanding. He'd had several run-ins with Queen Sora and it was now very pleasurable to see her afraid of her own shadow. "For the record," he announced, "I had nothing to do with the alleged hate event of last night."

"The fuck you don't," Harpy shrieked, having used the intervening moments to refill her lungs with air. "It's all connected. It intersects. The Resistance spells it all out on their website!"

"I'd be happy to debate you on that."

"I don't want to debate! I want to talk about my pain! Can nobody here understand that?"

"Friends, friends," Sora was unable to think of anything else to say because despite her advanced degrees in values she was suddenly feeling confused on whether she was actually herself a very good person with very good values. And she should never have agreed to the student shadow program. It was inevitable they would find out about the monopoly on poco and start causing—

"'Friends'? 'Friends'?" screamed a second-year student whose Instagram live feed of this event was earning him dozens of new followers, "I have friends who can't bear to live here anymore! From last night, to this, they're not doing their homework, they're losing sleep, skipping meals. They feel unsafe. They're breaking down. They're *breaking down!* Some of them couldn't even make it to the Teach-In!"

"That's really not normal," the Colonel said calmly. This statement was surprisingly credible considering it was uttered by a student named Alfred E. Neuman wearing a Confederate uniform and calling himself the Colonel of Truth.

"Not normal!" the lackeys chortled.

"He used the N-word!" someone screamed. "That's against the Virtue Code! You're the Dean! Punish him! *Pun-ish-him!*"

"Shhh," Sora had now transitioned to wondering whether that position in Oxford might still be available. "Please, friends, we do not use that word here." She had herself authored the campus legislation banning it, as well as the subsequent legislation, still pending, banning the phrase, "the N-word."

"Call it whatever," the Colonel said. "But Jeebus, it's fucked up. We live in warm comfortable lodges with grand pianos in our common rooms. Our courtyards have hammocks and picnic tables. Our bedrooms and suites have high-speed wi-fi and 200 cable TV channels. Our campus has computer labs, dance studios, a state-of-the-art gym, a professional quality theater and its own movie theater. An art gallery. We're served food that is ridiculously good, even if they are about to ruin that with the stupid vegan policy. And we can get that food any time we want, with all-night snack bars that deliver to our comfortable rooms. But you, you and your friends, you feel unsafe here, you can't bear to live here, in a place most people would kill to be, because someone puts on a piece of clothing? That's more than 'keeping it crazy,' I'd say. That's more than just ignoranosity. I'd say that's really fucked up."

"What's about to get fucked up is you, you racist piece of shit," someone in the crowd said, pushing forward along with the harpies.

The Colonel tensed up, as did his lackeys.

Sora collected herself—wondering whether the Virtue Code had a clear position on whether violence in support of the Virtue Code was itself virtuous—and moved over to the Emergency button that Harpy had threatened to press earlier. "Friends, please, it need not, it must not, come to this."

She stood poised with her finger at the button. She noticed, with a start, that there was a caterpillar crawling on the button. But she did not have to press it after all, for no sooner had she threatened to than the siren went off anyway.

Well not the siren, exactly. It was a long drawn-out call, coming over the campus speakers, heard at every spot on campus as if coming from every spot on campus. A deep bellowing sound, a soulful sound, a sound announcing a revelation or a rapture, an armaggedon or apocalypse, a first or second coming, accompanied by lightning and thunder, fire and brimstone, distant shouts and screams, haunting, existential, marking either the immediate presence or the utter absence of a divine being. No one was quite sure what the sound was or how it was produced but rumors ran from an enormous conch shell to an enormous ram's horn to some enormously complex computer program, and when it sounded at every spot on campus as from every spot on campus everyone stopped what they were doing, longed immediately either to die or to live on forever, and then understood.

It was time for the all-community gathering.

18

MEANWHILE TROUBLE WAS BREWING elsewhere.

Ezequiell was trying to figure these American kids out. For one, they insisted on calling him Zeke because it was easier to pronounce even though he insisted that his name was Ezequiell. More importantly they led these comfortable lives yet complained constantly of their discomfort. They didn't ever do any real work yet complained about their stress. They displayed no serious attachment to their family or their country but complained they felt isolated and lonely. They claimed to reject religion yet pursued their bizarre causes with almost religious zeal. Even the atheists in the "Be Grateful God is Dead Club"—whose meetings in the Lodge 2 basement he had checked out from a combination of curiosity and contempt—had developed rituals and festivals, namely singing along to loud psychedelic music after ingesting strong psychedelic drugs then consuming great quantities of munchies. With no interest in God or country or family these kids knew nothing about values and ethics and yet values and ethics was all they seemed to talk about, as if their quest (whatever it was for, exactly) was the noblest, and the only worthwhile, quest of them all.

To Zeke—damn, he was calling himself that now—this was all words, air. He himself came from a long and proud Argentinian gaucho tradition, had grown up on his family's cattle ranch in the Pampas, worked there until his *abuelo* finally sold the ranch to the corporation—don't get him started on that—but he had risen at dawn daily, worked hard, excelled in school, earned a scholarship to come study here because Nevergreen was supposedly so committed to internationalization. And then the first thing he learned after matriculating was that the school was considering going vegan in the name of social justice and to prevent cruelty to animals—in other words, that people here considered his family's traditional way of living as abominable and abolishable.

Imagine that. To privilege the stupid oversized lump of meat that was a cow over the long, proud tradition of hard-working and devout human beings. With that mindset it was no surprise they'd complain about how difficult and stressful their easy, do-nothing lives were. When he first had these realizations a few days after arrival here, he had been standing shirtless before the mirror in his lodge room, filming himself as he stiffened his bare broad dark-skinned chest and flexed his enormous biceps, themselves quite impressive oversized lumps of meat, he thought.

So Zeke's first order of business, that first week on campus last year, was to found the Carnivores Club. "No Beef With Beef!" said his first flyers, which he had paid for with his own money after the *Clarion* declined to run his ad. "Plants: What Food Eats!" was another.

Happily not everyone at the asylum was crazy.

A handful of meat-eaters turned up to the first meeting. That handful became two handfuls at the next meeting. A third handful joined by the end of the year.

The joy they took in rubbing their meat-rubs in the faces of all the pansies on campus. The stink they put up during those all-community gatherings where the proposal to go vegan was discussed. The pleasure they took in leaving slabs of decaying raw meat around campus with little signs saying, "Something Is Rotten On This Campus."

But then this semester those pansies had actually passed their cowshit legislation through the student council and then last month's gathering.

"Those pansies!" one meat-eater exclaimed to begin this

afternoon's meeting of the Club, which had been called to finally decide their tactics moving forward. The unfortunate delay was due to the fact that two of their members, both being sexually ravaged by Zeke on a nearly nightly basis, had fallen into a jealous dispute and couldn't stand to be in the same room; a dispute just recently resolved when Zeke moved on to nightly ravaging of a different member of the group.

"PETA, PETA, pumpkin-eaters!" exclaimed another meateater, proud of that clever slur against their primary campus nemesis. He was also proud of ignoring the Dean of Community Values's request for both sides to refrain from such slurs, in her office's failed attempt to mediate their campus dispute by getting them to jointly focus instead on major human rights issues in the Middle East.

"And what about *human* rights?" exclaimed a third, speaking of human rights. "Don't we have rights too?"

Zeke scratched his nails on the wall to make a horrendous screeching sound. Everyone cringed, and all eyes turned to him as he brought the meeting to order.

"Let's flay the motherfuckers," Zeke said.

"Wait, flay or filet?" a carnivore asked who sometimes had trouble with Zeke's accent.

"Both," Zeke said, "those motherfuckers."

There was a long silence as the carnivores felt both yearning and fear in front of their muscled leader, as his fingertips had just dug grooves into concrete walls. The sound reverberated as powerfully as his baritone-bass voice, as their meetings were in the music rehearsal area with the amazing acoustics on the fifth floor of the Adorno Center. They had scored this highly coveted Area 51 for their meetings ever since Zeke had scored with the music department's administrative assistant.

"So what do we do, boss?" one newly joined meat-eater asked, a handsome young fellow with a freshly scrubbed face sporting little round glasses and big round biceps nearly rivaling those of their leader.

"We already have The Spit," another meat-eater said, the barbecue stand's primary manager.

"We have already announced our plan to roast and eat the caterpillars when they come out," another said, who was willing to do whatever his leader wanted him to do, starting with the caterpillar he had already roasted and consumed that morning in a test run.

"And we already came out in support of climate change!" a last said, referring to last year's stormy campus debate about the meteorological consequences of cattle flatulence. "What's left, Zeke?"

"Men," Zeke said, again commanding attention. There were in fact three female members of the group, but they were actually rather aroused by their leader's referring to them this way; either during their group meetings, or while they were, individually or together, being ravaged by him. "What do they say they object to, exactly?"

"Destruction of the rain forest."

"Displacement of indigenous people."

"The farts, the methane. Climate change."

"Yes," Zeke said, "and we have already stated our support for all those things. But you are missing the most basic, the most fundamental, the thing that is in plain sight."

There was a long silence as they tried to work it out. Finally, one of the male-presenting students, admiring the way Zeke's chest swelled whenever he spoke about destroying the rain forest, saw what their leader was aiming at.

"The cruelty," he said, breathing deeply.

"Exactly," Zeke said, his chest swelling.

"So we support cruelty to animals now?" a more timid meat-eater asked.

"We have always supported cruelty to animals!" Zeke snapped. "We just have refrained from practicing it."

"You mean …?"

"Yes …" Zeke answered, slowly. "The *piglets*."

The room was dead silent, except for a low moan in the rear.

"Since I arrived here last year," Zeke said, many of his muscles stiffening, "these pansies have been attacking us, assaulting us, trying, as it were—to hunt us down. Well, men." He paused again, just long enough for two of the female meat-eaters, and one of the males, to climax. "Tonight, the hunted," he exhaled, "become the hunters. You—" he pointed at the newly joined carnivore, "may fetch my body paint."

At that moment the conch or ram's horn or voice of God blasted through the speakers in the room, demanding their attendance at the all-community gathering.

19

The Roswell Crypt was the largest space on campus.

Buried in the center of the upper campus directly beneath the Maze, the deep round hollow was the only space on campus that could accommodate nearly all of the students and faculty. Originally dug by the indigenous people of the island for storing their dead, it was preserved out of respect by those who later came and slaughtered them all, then stashed them there alongside their ancestors. Its geological properties—in particular its remarkable dryness, given that it was on an island—made it perfect for preserving the mummified remains, still dressed in undecaying native garb. Later the founders of the asylum built their central observation tower above it, inspired by the Millbank Prison being constructed in London at that time, itself inspired by the English philosopher Jeremy Bentham. Bentham, widely known for the utilitarian idea that you should produce the most pleasure for the most people, was less widely known for the idea that this was best achieved by producing the most surveillance by the fewest people. Thus was born the "panopticon," an institutional system of control in which all the inmates could be observed, or at least think they were being observed, by even a single watchman in a central watchtower. This worked terrifically at the asylum until the riots of 1846, when the inmates expressed their opposition to their incarceration by murdering the observers all along the watchtower and then burning the whole thing down. Instead of rebuilding the tower the survivors instead planted the scarred earth with the hedges making up the Maze, and the Moondial was built in the middle as a memorial to the staff and inmates who died during the riots. The Crypt beneath was undisturbed by the excitement, and remained unchanged until it was renovated by the Roswell family shortly after the infamous insect infestation of 1921, in gratitude for the care administered to five generations of crazy Roswells. Their only strange requirement was that the renovated space should resemble the Roman Colosseum (or so the current Conspiracy Club claimed), and so it was used (they also claimed) for gladiatorial contests, theatrical farces, and criminal executions.

Today, it seemed, it was to be used for all three at once.

The place was near capacity, warm, the electric torches sprinkled throughout adding several degrees to the steaming heat of the human bodies. Time was when the idea of a "mandatory" community meeting was anathema: back in the 1960s and 1970s you could sooner herd a mass of feral cats than get faculty and students to accept a command to assemble. But today the student shadows had met almost no resistance in encouraging their assigned faculty and administration members to attend; the student facilitators leading class discussions about combating hate in all its forms had barely had to explain that anyone who failed to attend the gathering, and thus failed to affirm their Community Values, was someone who failed to hate hate, and thus was a hater themself.

And there were no haters here, they would permit no haters here, for here, only, were the haters of hate.

It's so beautiful, thought Ariana, now in her fourth year as she stood (as there were no seats) in the third level up from the bottom circle, furiously sipping pomo from her Nevergreen-logo'd water bottle and getting excited about what was to come. What a contrast to her first days on campus! She had arrived here rather dubious. To be honest, Nevergreen was her last choice because she knew the place was "different," and if there was one thing she knew she was, it was solidly normal. Even after she did not get into her other schools she was resistant, too filled with resentment that people like her, people who could trace their ancestry all the way back, were being shut out of places and replaced by, you know, *others*, to imagine she might be satisfied here. It was only when her father informed her during her monthly visit to him—*totally* trumped up charges, by the way, all he had done was what any patriot would do to defend his people—that while Nevergreen's "crazy" thing meant it would be filled up with undesirables, it did have one advantage: there were no more of *those people* here, who were responsible for the "progress" destroying her people's way of life and replacing her people with, you know, others, *those people* who were the truest haters of all things and people noble and virtuous. And okay, so those other undesirables hated her and her friends in her student club for hating them (her club of which she was now President, by the way); but she and her friends also hated *them* for hating *them*, as it were, so maybe they really weren't all so different after all, in their mutual hatred of haters? So yes she had come here skeptical, but now in her fourth year, with the absence of *those people*, along with the kick-ass pomo and with her ass-kicking friends, she was feeling committed to this place, to this beautiful moment, feeling her heart filling with hatred along with those of her closest friends—or rather, with hatred of hatred. And what could be better, she thought, so alert, her heart racing, than hating hate with close friends?

Ah, it was beginning.

That small but powerful woman, Prof. Piece or something, had descended to the bottom circle and taken her position in the spotlight at the podium.

"May we come to order, please," she asked, to no effect.

A disturbance had broken out near the top. Carrying over the dispute from this morning's Expo, the members of the First World Club had attempted to take over the spots assigned to the Third World Club, or the latter had tried to eject the former from the gathering altogether; it was impossible to reconcile the competing narratives. Either way, Vice Dean Luiz's subversion of boss Sora's Expo arrangement plan continued to produce the pushing and shoving that would suggest to the Elders that Sora was unsuited for her job. "You need to back off, respect the students' space," Peace was urging into the microphone, though to whom, precisely, was not clear, since they were all students. When that was met by only increased disturbance, she said more forcefully, "Who wants to help me get these people out of here? I need some muscle over here!" It took several minutes but the Virtue Patrol was able to secure the peace, for Peace.

"Come to order, please," Peace repeated, now feeling the excitement.

She was not sure of the details but was pleased to receive friend Luiz's message that friend Sora was unavailable to fulfill her duty here, and was bursting not with pride (since pride was not a virtue) but with some virtuous mode of pride that she had been designated with the awesome responsibility of fostering the universal hatred of hate. This time her request was adequately followed.

"We shall begin here," she continued, "in this holiest of holy places, with a moment. A moment to reflect on our values. A moment to remember and honor those noble messengers, and martyrs, of our values, those warriors for peace whose legacy would make all of us so proud, were pride not proscribed by those same values. And a moment, on this day, to reflect on our desire that, perhaps, one day, our lost brothers and sisters and others may choose to come back. Dr. Fester," she turned to that illuminatus seated next to her in the center of the circle, "will you lead us in our silence?"

The round old man continued to gaze forward in the spotlight focused on his face as a moment of near silence descended upon the audience, partly in memory but also partly in shock that friend Peace had spoken the unspeakable and made reference to The Episode. Ariana herself also felt shock, but at the expressed desire that *those people* come back. As for the "messengers" and "martyrs," Peace was speaking of the All You Need is Love Club from some years ago. The pacifist student group, inspired by yet another war over there, had decided to put theory into practice, raised some funds, and headed off to the Middle East to preach their universal message, and promptly been slaughtered by combatants from all sides of every conflict there. "Maybe You Also Need a Gun" was the callous slogan coined after by the Happiness is a Warm Gun student club in protest against the campus deification of the martyred pacifists. The deep wound inflicted on Nevergreen's collective psyche by these events in turn triggered The Episode, and while they did regularly remember the noble student pacifists, they largely preferred not to remember the less noble consequences.

The silence lingered and the spotlight dimmed to darkness. But then, softly, quietly at first but then increasing in volume, angelic voices began permeating the room, one by one. Targeted spotlights revealed members of the a cappella group Universal Harmony descending down different ramps toward the bottom circle, in their mindfully designed costumes and mindfully choreographed sequence: the first member in the all red vineyard vines button-down striped shirt and short shorts and faux-leather boat shoes, the second in the all orange vineyard vines the same, and so on, in the sequence of colors of that universal symbol of universal harmony, the rainbow. As they descended they were slowly singing, chanting, the most haunting version of *All You Need Is Love* you will ever hear, as a dirge, a lament: "All … you … need … is … love … dun … dun … dun … dun … dun …" As they came together on the bottom, unfurling their rainbow in the bottom circle, they were singing louder, almost a climax, "All you need is love, love," concluding with the repeating echo, "love is all you need, love is all you need, love is all you need …" and slowly fading away as the spotlights faded and the dark and the silence resumed, which in turn soon yielded to the snapping of hundreds of sets of fingers in the darkness.

But then this expression of universal approval was itself penetrated first by some jeering from somewhere and then by another disturbance in a circle roughly halfway up. The Pro-Life Club had really had it up to here. The ridicule, the mocking, this they were used to, but their opposition to the new vegan policy, since it amounted to institutional vegicide, had recently resulted in other students pelting them with murdered vegetables. Then their face mask campaign to halt the ongoing microbicide of ordinary respiration had gotten two of their members beaten up. But now this! The Pro-Choice Club, assigned to stand next to them today, began taunting them with their own new platform, that the scope of "choice" should be expanded from fetuses to living children up to the age of twelve. The only positive thing about their being located adjacent to each other, the Pro-Lifers thought, was that it made the punching that much easier.

"And now," Peace continued once the Virtue Patrol had again secured the peace, "the reason we are here today. What we are about to hear is difficult, will be difficult, to hear; and those who cannot bear it are invited to make use of the comfort spaces established above," she referred to the tents set up outside, with soft cushions and milk and cookies, "but if we are to oppose hate, if we are to truly hate hate, then we must—see it, hear it, confront it, head on. And please note: Cardboard notions of civility need not restrain the discussion when our goal, our need, is to hear each individual's open, honest truth. Please, with respect, may we hear from our first witness."

Pomo was in the air, student phones were filming, likes and hearts and adorable emojis were accumulating from those not fortunate to be present at this historic event, and the testimonies began.

"My name is Baara," the first young woman exclaimed, standing in the spotlight at the center of the circle. "I am in my first year of ripening here. Y'all hear me out there?"

"Baara! Baara!" the crowd murmured.

"Here, me," she announced, pointing at herself, "so hear me! I believe in free speech, but I am here to tell y'all how hate hurts. That man, who challenged everything, every *thing*, we hold dear ..."

"Hear, hear!" the crowd murmured, or perhaps "here, here";

no one was clear, not that it mattered, since they didn't really need to hear the two-minutes of details, how given what she had learned in these first nine weeks of her political science fiction class it followed that last night's lecturer had assaulted their fundamental principles, the freedom, the autonomy, the mutual respect for sameness and for difference, the acceptance of all things and their opposites, that underlay everything good at Nevergreen. They knew it all already, and in any case, why waste attention on details when, in the dark and in the pomo-infused air, there was so much good making out available with your neighboring students? And there were even several mattresses lying around here …

"My hero!" proclaimed Professor A. M. Alek of the Near East Languages and Literature department as he hugged Baara afterward, having deliberately stood in the bottom circle to more easily praise and touch each witness.

"My name is Keziah!" the second speaker exclaimed, the second first-year-ripener on the roster.

"Keziah! Keziah!" the crowd murmured.

"I believe in free speech, but that man last night—" Keziah paused, inhaled, then screamed, "sexually assaulted me!" The crowd gasped appropriately, madly punching the hashtag #HerToo into their live-stream commentary, not really needing the two-minutes of details to be horrified as she borrowed terminology gleaned from any number of classes to explain how certain words having nothing whatever to do with sexuality can, when uttered in the right gentle way by the right sort of unassuming person, constitute extreme sexual violence toward a person not actually present.

"My hero!" proclaimed Prof. Alek, as he hugged.

"Dudes! Dudettes!" bellowed the first second-year student to the podium, wearing the royal crimson t-shirt and forgetting the instruction to state his name and degree of indoctrination. "I bam ba lam believe in free speech! But I ask you, my dudes, I ask you, my dudettes—who shall speak for the purple piper? Who shall speak for the black queen? I ask you, now: Who shall speak for the *yellow jester?!*"

"*We* shall!" the crowd shouted, confusing the poor fellow who had assumed they would all join him in proclaiming, "the Crimson King!" Not that it mattered, because they were too busy cultivating their hatred of hate to listen to his two-minutes diatribe about the death of music since the late 1970s, or whatever it was he was diatribing about. Nor were they paying much attention to the next second-year ripener, who was stunning in his bright yellow sari but impossible to follow with his topological proofs of the speaker's hateful hating and hatred.

"I am ... the Lieutenant of Truth!" exclaimed a third-year on the roster, his eyes darting frantically around the darkened circles of the room, hoping that that girl Keziah was still around. There was no danger that that tyrant the Colonel would be here—they were supposed to boycott the gathering, since they objected to every aspect of it starting with the "mandatory"—but he also couldn't be sure that the Colonel hadn't sent any of his spies. He was starting to think that almost everyone here was a spy, in fact, including some of his fellow members of the Conspiracy Club. But God, it felt good to call himself the Lieutenant ...

"Diatribe! Diatribe!" the crowd demanded, their attention span ill suited for the seconds of silence elapsed since the Lieutenant came to the podium.

"I speak for ... the Truth!" he exclaimed, rising to the occasion, literally, by standing on his toes for some reason. He had been following Keziah for weeks now and thought here was his chance to impress her ... "I affirm the principle of free speech, but that man last night," he explained, had attacked not just values but standards, not just standards but norms, not just norms but objectivity, not just objectivity but subjectivity, and so not just truth (with a small t) but Truth (with a capital T), and so on, and so forth. The crowd didn't follow this one either, although there was some appreciative applause when he said "and so on, and so forth," thus indicating he was coming to a close.

"He blinked! He blinked!" someone shouted, as Dr. Taslitz M. Fester had done just that in the spotlight, producing a great roar in the crowd.

And so it went, three members of each of the major ripening cohorts spent two minutes each affirming freedom of speech but condemning hate in all its forms, the hate that hurts, the hate that is violence, the hate that abuses the freedom of speech, and so on and so forth. Ariana soaked it all in: the speeches, her peers, the look of not-pride in Peace's eyes, the silent deep gaze of Dr. Fester in his wheelchair, the impassioned cries of "my hero!" from Prof. Alek (who she already admired from what she had heard about his role in The Episode). She was loving it all (okay except for that weird kid who called himself the Lieutenant and had sort of stalked her all last year), and she knew, just knew, that she had to share her pain as well. When Peace returned to the podium she had barely finished saying, "And would anyone else care to share their pain?" when Ariana was at the microphone sharing her pain.

"My name is Ariana, and I am fourth year, and I believe in free speech," she began, trembling, and then could not stop as she thought about *those people* and their hatred, "but I hate hate speech, and I hate hate silence, and I hate hate!" The crowd's murmur turned to a roar as she testified to her pain, the pain of being a minority, of knowing she and her people were exceptional yet so few in number, outnumbered, of being denied the privileges that others took for themselves when it was her people who deserved them, the privileges that specific others took, cheated, stole, from her people, that even this administration echoed at times, when some of these people, these Fat Cats, these backstabbers, these parasites, got to enjoy this *elixir*, the "poco," when the rest of them had to make do with pomo, only pomo, delicious and stimulating as this was, it was the principle, the chosen few who on the backs of all the rest kept the poco only for themselves—

"My hero!" proclaimed Prof. Alek as he embraced Ariana,

feeling the pain that Ariana had been so brave to share and also her shapely pure-blooded womanly body.

"Po-co, po-co!" Ariana began to chant as she squirmed from Prof. Alek, riling the crowd, which began to chant with her, "Po-co! Po-co!"

The single spotlight illuminating her hate-hating face flickered, perilously close to going out.

The crowd roared louder, "Po-co! Po-co!"

The cable, Peace thought. That damn cable could not go out again right now, not when the energy was cresting, when the power structures were poised to fall, they had to act fast. She looked at Dr. Fester, took his blink as a signal to turn to Corrie, who was standing nearby, waiting, and flashed the V signal. Corrie rushed to the podium as the Virtue Patrol pried Prof. Alek from Ariana again and returned them to their spots. There was further mayhem along the upper circle as the Anti-Marshmallow Club, driven to a frenzy by the stirring testimony, finally commenced the long overdue beating of the Marshmallow Club members assigned to the spaces next to them. While the Virtue Patrol went to secure the peace over there, too, Corrie went to undermine the peace everywhere else.

"Friends, friends, friends," Corrie said quietly as the spotlight flickered once more, then resumed reflecting in her severe eyes. She began to read the script that the Resistance had given her. "We come to the end. But the end is the beginning. The beginning of the end!"

She didn't quite know what this meant, nor did anyone else, but they all roared in approval anyway. Some in the lower circles thought they saw Dr. Fester blink again and roared even louder.

"Lower the Panoramicon!" the Resistance commanded, through Corrie.

Every making-out face disengaged from every other and turned to look; every phone stopped filming Corrie and instead turned toward the ceiling of the Crypt, from which was now descending that technological marvel, the enormous 360-degree circular

LED screen which was also the last major non-administrative purchase by the college before the budget cuts. Inspired by the asylum's original panopticon tower, this device was designed not for doing the watching but for being watched.

"To help us prepare for our collective two minutes of hating hate, our Two-Minute Hate-Hate," Corrie said solemnly, having memorized this part, "indeed to help us focus our energy on the hate we must hate, I present to you, my dear fellow haters of hate, the face of hate."

The photo Corrie had snapped during the Clubs Expo earlier in the day now appeared in full 360-degree glory on the Panoramicon. There was J.'s face, slightly puffy, slightly haggard, with sinister shadows darkened upon an awkward tense expression of confusion and maybe fear, one of his eyelids caught half-closed, his nose blurred and shadowed almost like a snout, and possibly, possibly, with a bit of spittle hanging from the corner of his mouth. The photoshopping had really brought out the inner sinister, Corrie thought, admiring her work, thinking to herself: this was no little piggie, but the Big Pig himself, and it was she who had exposed him.

In the dark hall with the spotlight on her face, hers in contrast the face of virtue, Corrie paused, soaked it in, soaked it up, then narrowed her severe eyes and spoke.

"Let our hatred of hate begin!" the Resistance exclaimed through her and the crowd broke into angry, furious, terrifying roars.

PART IV

KILL THE BEAST! CUT HIS THROAT!
SPILL HIS BLOOD!

20

AT THAT VERY INSTANT that same face was displaying roughly the same confusion and fear, with one of its eyelids caught half-open and a bit of spittle hanging from its mouth, minus the blurring and sinister shadows, and snoring blissfully ignorantly in the last dying sliver of sunlight on a patch of grass in the lower campus Eternal Sanctuary. J. had stirred uneasily a few minutes before, at the same time as the power had flickered, but then returned to his dream: He and Debra were shopping for burial plots. There were so many options, choices, decisions, above ground, below, cremating, no not that, at least they agreed on that. But there was a sale, buy one get one half off, but even better J. thought, maybe they could just share one, one plot, one coffin even, the two of them, wouldn't that be sort of, I don't know, romantic?

Are you crazy? Debra said.

I am, but how is that relevant? J. said. Don't you want to share a plot with me? You know, sort of romantic?

I don't even like sharing a bathroom with you, Debra said back. Why would I want to share eternity in a little box with you?

Just then a cool breeze crossed his face and he, and his dreams, shifted. The brochure in his jacket pocket explained that the sanctuary had been designed in the last century under the theory that a carefully controlled wilderness would have a calming effect on the out-of-control wilderness of the inmates themselves. And indeed J. had come here seeking that calming effect after what he had witnessed in the hours preceding. He had wavered about the Teach-In, even with Thatch's pointing out that no one would

113

recognize him. But both Robert and Thatch had gone to teach however many students might show up to their 3:00 PM classes, his texts to Brenda had had no reply, there were hours to the next ferry, and he was still refraining from calling home so he literally had nothing to do anyway. So when another small tourist group wandered by, J., comforted by the additional anonymity the group provided, joined in. That he was no longer thinking entirely clearly was evidenced by the fact that the tourists were Japanese.

"Here we have another example of Nevergreen's famous approach to 'Engaged Learning'," the student tour guide was saying to the four of them, walking backward as she led them into the lounge. She was wearing the official t-shirt of the campus tea shop, Chai Guevara, featuring the iconic image of the revolutionary leader sipping a mug of chai itself emblazoned with the Chai Guevara logo. "This week's Teach-In is all about free speech and hate speech."

"This week's?" one tourmate asked in an adequate English, snapping a photo of the lounge as they entered.

"Oh yes! Engaged Learning is Real Time Learning. It's about engaging with the issues of the day, the week, the hour."

"What was last week's Teach-In about?"

"Well, that was about hate speech and free speech."

"Isn't that the same topic?"

"Hardly! The order is totally different. Ah, here's the first session. Please be quiet so we can listen for a little."

They listened to a student talking about "How Hate Hurts." To blend in J. took some pictures, trying not to think about the fact that the student was pretty clearly speaking about him.

"Aren't there professors here? If there is teaching?" another tourmate asked, filming the student tour guide as she answered.

"Professors are pressured to attend the Teach-Ins, of course," she bobbed her head to offer her best look to the camera, "but at Nevergreen we believe that Learning is Teaching. Since too much education actually diminishes knowledge, the teaching here is done, as much as possible, by the students. Now," she said, bobbing one last time for the camera, "try shooting me from this angle."

But J. had already gone, having had enough of this section. He moved past some students wearing t-shirts to protest the extreme reverence given to some apparently martyred student pacifists. Was it really necessary, they complained, to commemorate those idiots at every college event? Was it really necessary to inflict Universal Harmony's dour version of *All You Need is Love* on them again and again? J. glimpsed the front of the shirts: the slogan, "Love Is The Answer," was written above a photo of the smiling student pacifists as they were boarding the plane to the Middle East. As J. passed he turned to see the backs of the shirts, with the slogan, "But To What Question?" written above images of the activists' butchered bodies.

This distasteful sight proved a good segue to the next panel, J. thought, feeling a little unwell, lingering there long enough to learn that pretty much all the violence in the world was due to the very hate speech that had assaulted their campus the night before. In desperate need of a respite J. left the lounge and made his way back down the hill to the Eternal Sanctuary, to kill the time until the ferry. "Sounds relaxing," J. had responded when Robert suggested, over their sausage lunch, that he spend a little time there.

"Yes, darling," Thatch had answered, "you may surely rest in peace there. Like the others."

"What does that mean?" J. asked.

"People go in, darling. They don't always come out."

"Conspiracy Club rumors," Robert elaborated. "Mostly false. The last alleged disappearance was, what, Thatch?"

"Was it three years ago, darling? It was that insane student trying to turn himself into a reptile. Had his tongue split, scales grafted to his skin. Ate mice. That sort of thing."

"My money is he drowned trying to swim off the island," Robert speculated. "Either that or eaten by the piglets. Otherwise his body would have been found."

Having his body not be found, at least for a while, sounded appealing to J. as he entered the sanctuary. He paused, listened, thought he could hear shouts and murmurs from the upper campus; was that a—what was the name of that thing—*vuvuzuela* in the distance? Whatever it was he quickened his step the opposite direction, moving onto the first trail he found. He hadn't mentioned at lunch that the brochure confirmed that one of the first professors at the college, a Prof. of Positive Science and Mental Hygiene named Ernest Netzach, had indeed disappeared in these woods, in this wilderness, his body never found; perhaps that was the little germ of truth that fueled the later rumors. Germ of truth, J. thought, following the half-overgrown trail more deeply into the woods; a nice idea, that, imagining truth (like old age!) being contagious, spreading, maybe producing an epidemic. Thinking about that he imagined coming upon Prof. Netzach's body, what would be left of it decades letter, a pile of bones; unless bones too would decay in the elements? Far more likely he would come upon more recent remains, the reptile-student, if it was only three years ago the flesh would be gone but who knows what the scales were made of, something synthetic, perhaps he would come upon a pile of bones and scales …

J. felt the chill. His thin jacket was not much protection against the fall weather, and with the sun on the decline, the shadows deepening, his thoughts themselves darkening … He pulled his jacket a little tighter then pulled out his phone, but of course there was no reception here, in these woods, as there was barely any reception on this island. He started wondering if Debra would even miss him if he disappeared here. The three monsters were half grown up already and barely grunted at him in the morning, they probably didn't even realize he was away, in fact recently he and Debra had been sort of bantering about separating and he had said, jokingly, I'm not sure I would fight you for custody and she had said why would you, you barely have custody now. They had both laughed but that actually stung, that remark, it wasn't at all true but why would she say that, his wife, his wife who didn't want to spend eternity too close to him, would she even notice if he never came back …

Somewhere in the distance he heard that long painful sound commanding everyone to the gathering. It was far away, he was far away, lost even, the darkness coming on, in his thoughts. He shivered again. There was a clearing ahead. A lovely field, really, with grass somewhat groomed, and most of all illuminated by the last broad shaft of light from the dying sun. The air, and his mood, lightened slightly as he found a patch to lie down on, rest. He noticed, as he settled in, another mound of pig-droppings nearby, having again failed to step in it for the good luck he sorely could use. On reflection he was not so fond of this "germ of truth" idea, no, not when the truth was unpleasant, when the truth was dark, chilly, the eternal solitude of a lonely tomb, the scattered bones abandoned by flesh, a reptile-boy floundering in the swirling currents swallowing the island ...

It was with these thoughts that J. fell into the sanctuary of sleep, an initially dreamless sleep, thankfully. It was in this dreamless sleep that he was unaware of what was brewing in the all-community gathering. It was in this dreamless sleep that he stirred, slightly, during that strange electromagnetic moment disturbing the power flow to, and through, the asylum. But with that strange moment the dreamless sleep began to yield, a drop of spittle escaping the corner of his mouth as the last sliver of light on his face was breathing its last and as, a short distance away, a two-minute horde of hatred was being directed at that same face. He started dreaming about Wound Man, how often lately he dreamed about Wound Man, a medieval trope from the fifteenth century but which remained in use, in anatomy books and surgical texts, well into the seventeenth. The artists were unknown but clearly working from each other, the dia-grams, often full color portraits, showing the back and front of the body and the internal muscles and organs, illustrating, for the barber surgeon, or just the curious, the many types of inju-ries a human being could suffer. Thus inserted into poor Wound Man was an assortment of arrows, swords, knives, the occasional axe, sometimes you might find a dog or a snake or a scorpion biting the poor fellow's leg or feet. And not just inserted into him but buried into him, the knife to the hilt, the arrow to the feathers, spurts of blood coming out of the wound, with detailed illustrations of the shredded muscles and organs within. J. had taught himself Latin to read the captions describing the injuries and recommending the medical responses. But most fascinating of all was Wound Man's expression. Though the unknown artists did it differently they all represented his face not as one of someone undergoing unimaginable pain, not as someone in the throes of dying, but as someone resigned to his fate or maybe even bored. So J. was dreaming of Wound Man, dreaming of Wound Man's face, until in his dream of course Wound Man's face slowly morphed, became *his* face. J. felt hollow, hollow in his heart, somehow looking at his face on Wound Man's body while at the same time looking out from that face, looking down, seeing the knives and spears and arrows buried into him …

It was at that moment that, not so far away, the chief hater-of-hate, Big Chief Hater-of-Hate, both not-proud and a little afraid of the intensity she had unleashed, and the Resistance had unleashed, unleashed an army of hate-haters into the world. Thus was J. somewhere in the woods wrestling with internal demons when a horde of external demons was spilling out from the gathering, the Crypt was discharging, vomiting, from all its orifices, on all sides of the Maze it was spewing up and out its germs of hatred-haters by the hundreds, in search of hatred to hate. But if Wound Man now resembled J. so too did these agents of hatred, as they were all wearing the masks that Big Chief Corrie had had made from the photograph, the large masks with J.'s face on them with sinister slits cut for their eyes within the sinister shadows of his eyes in the photo, the masks handed to them as they were expelled into the environment, streamed into every hexant and beyond, hollering and whooping and signaling their V for virtue signs, their V for Wagner's "Valkyries" that was pumping all over from the campus speakers. Mixing right in with them as they spread out were some students who hadn't needed the gathering to get themselves riled up, who had spent that time stripping down to loincloths (and breastcloths for the females), war-painting their faces and chests (and breasts), and who were now frightening even themselves a little as they ran down the hill to the lower campus screaming, "Kill the beast! Cut its throat! Spill its blood!"

And so J. was just sinking into his lonesome wound-filled dream when the denizens of Nevergreen, having had their fill of hating hate in the abstract, began streaming out of the Crypt in search of hate in the concrete.

Just then he felt that awful thing, that scratching, that clawing, on his face.

21

"Aaahhh!" he screamed, scratching, clawing at his face, tearing away not one but two thick caterpillars crawling on his upper lip and the side of his nose respectively. He flung them away as he bolted upright, not even stopping to think that where there were two caterpillars there were likely to be more. There was no time to think this because, now awake, his attention was instantly drawn elsewhere.

"Kill the beast! Cut his throat! Spill his blood!" These awful shouts were coming from the woods at the edge of the clearing, accompanied by violent stamping through the underbrush. It was hard to locate them exactly, since he was barely awake and the dusk was so heavy. When had the sun gone down? How long had he been asleep? Where was he? In the near pitch-dark, in the woods, the sanctuary—

"Cut his throat!" the shouts came close by, louder stamping.

He dropped back down into the grass, willed himself to be invisible. Thank goodness for the dusk he thought, obscuring him, blanketing him, as he could just make out the group of intimidating young people marching almost right by him, bright white war paint on their faces and bodies and brandishing long sticks whittled down to sharp points. Were those—*spears?* What the hell had he done—

"Spill his blood!" they chanted as they disappeared back into the woods, having just missed him. For a moment J. began to relax, a long moment in which he was not in the woods in the dark being hunted by frenzied lunatics, a moment that ended abruptly when said lunatics began ululating nearby. Horrid, shrieking, guttural sounds, animal sounds, *bloodthirsty.*

Better get out of here, wherever exactly here was.

"Damn it!" he muttered as he got up and put his foot down immediately adjacent to the pile of pig-droppings, again.

He ran as softly as he could the opposite way from the beast-hunters, re-entered the woods. After a bit he stopped to take his bearings, but then snorted at the idea of taking bearings in the darkness. Hadn't Robert mentioned a full moon tonight? Would it kill the moon to come out already, the dark was so heavy. Maybe the moon had come out but only the dark side, because it's all dark, what a strange time to think *that*, he thought. Of course he was lost, he would probably be lost even by moon-light so there was surely no hope in the dark. He was fairly sure the entrance to the sanctuary, and thus the exit, was—that way, roughly. Unless of course he had gotten turned around, in which case it would be the other way. How long had he been asleep, anyway? And the ferry, when was the ferry. He could check his phone but he didn't want to shine the light, lest he signal the— why were people dressed in war paint hunting here?

Hunting *him?*

He tried to listen, over the pounding of his heart.

The ululating had died away. There were some late fall crickets chirping somewhere but otherwise all seemed, well, *quiet.*

Something crashed out of the brush, squirreling past his feet, giving him a small heart attack. A much larger heart attack followed when he heard screams of "Kill the beast!" coming from much closer than he would have preferred. No longer bothering to keep his movements quiet he took off again away from the hunters. There was that period when Debra was trying to convince him to exercise more, or even a little, to get in better shape. That period was going on some twenty years now, and suddenly his many objections—at least he wasn't overweight, and weights are so damn heavy, and aerobic activities so tiring—seemed unpersuasive now that he was running through the woods pursued by ululating youths who wanted to skin the beast whose heart was pounding whose breath was haltering who didn't think he could run another step—

He stopped. He could not continue.

He couldn't breathe.

He heard his name being called.

"J.? Is that you?"

It was Robert.

"God am I glad to see you!" J. almost threw himself on the man standing at the entrance (and thus exit) of the sanctuary. "How did you find me?"

"I figured you'd come here. And then I heard the hyperventilating. My God look at you!" In the first light of the rising moon, or perhaps in the light of the guidestone by the sanctuary sign, Robert could see the sweat and the scratches.

"You'll never believe—"

"Oh I believe. I'm glad to see you too. This place is falling apart, even more than usual. Are you all right?"

J. realized he had been crying. "I'm fine."

"Good. For now. So listen."

"All ears."

"Let's go find some grown-ups. They'll meet and have poco and discuss. Then things will be all right."

"What?"

"I'm taking you back to the administration. They have responsibilities here and they've got to do something. Also," he added, "you may recall that you have an appointment."

J. stared at him blankly.

"Friend Aal was going to speak to the President," Robert reminded him. "To figure out how to deal with the Offensiveness Complaints. And now of course all this. I have come to fetch you. There is a non-zero possibility that everything will turn out all right."

J. willed himself to take a breath. Somewhere in the distant sanctuary they could hear ululating.

22

"AAL, I DON'T UNDERSTAND," Robert said. "I specifically requested that the President join us."

Vice President, and friend, Aaliyah remained firm. "Bob does not see the need, my dear. Bob said the wheels of virtue are turning just as they ought, and that we must be patient for them to produce their virtuous result. Bob worries, and I share that worry, that perhaps you are overreacting." Aal did not say it, but then again did not need to, for Robert to hear the word *again* appended to that sentence.

"But look at him," Robert indicated J. and his scratches.

"When Shawn gets here we shall confer on whether he needs some bandaids."

"Shawn? I specifically requested he *not* join us."

Aal laughed. "Oh, that is a good one, friend Robert. Now, for our esteemed visitor," she turned to J., "the team is here, the team is ready. How can we best support you, my dear?"

"You call this the team?" Robert interrupted. "The President is AWOL, and instead of Big Sister we've only got Little Brother here? And where's *your* little shadow, Little Bro?"

Vice Dean Luiz Bacharo was seated on an adjacent cushion, still chuckling about Robert's request about Shawn while twirling his hair. "'Big Sister,' as you say," Luiz tried to appear concerned, "has herself been AWOL since this afternoon. Vanished. Poof!" He snapped his fingers, barely concealing his glee. "My 'little shadow' is out there now, organizing search efforts. Any other questions, Prof. Bowtie?" My goodness how empowering that last little lie felt, Luiz was thinking, having given Harpya the evening off to enjoy the collective hatred. He should have started this campaign *long* ago.

And "Dean of Community Values" sure sounded nice, Luiz thought. Perhaps it was time to bring back those titles.

"I yield the floor," Robert sighed.

"Oh, dear," Aal said with genuine concern about her missing Dean, if they still used that title. "But I am afraid that finding dear friend Sora shall have to be tomorrow's mission. This evening's mission is about our esteemed visitor. So I ask again, my dear. How may we best support you?"

J., who hadn't minded not participating in this conversation, realized he now had to. "You can stop them—from attacking me," he said, with measured desperation.

"Attacking you?" Aal said.

"They're not attacking you," Luiz said.

"It's not about you," Aal said.

"Not about me?"

"Not at all." Luiz shook his hair.

"The OCs? That started all this off?" Robert asked. "Weren't they about him? And speaking of …?"

"Unresolved," Aal reported. "Bob says we must allow the wheels of virtue to turn."

"But that is directly about me," J. protested.

"A purely impersonal process," Luiz shook his hair again. "Rules, procedures, established independently, entirely out of our hands."

"Not at all about you, my dear," Aal said again.

"But what about this?" J. pulled out his phone to show them what Robert had shown him while they were waiting to be called in. There was the Resistance website, where he clicked on the newest headline, "Hate Comes to Nevergreen." He was intending to show her the latest article Cerise and Verisce had written about his hate-filled lecture from the night before.

Instead an image of his face came up.

He groaned, as much about the fact that his face was now officially out there as that the photo was so unflattering, with that eyelid half-closed. And was that some spittle at his mouth?

"Oh, that's not about you," Aal said.

"Not at all," Luiz added, blinking.

"But that's my face. It fills the entire screen."

"That's not your face, my dear," Aal objected. "At most a resemblance. Your face shadows are barely half as sinister."

"Almost definitely not you," Luiz agreed. "They probably just took that off the internet. That's probably just somebody photo-shopped to look like you. And even if it were you, it symbolizes something else entirely."

J. couldn't follow his logic. "I think they're trying to kill me! They were screaming 'Kill the beast!' when they came into the sanctuary for me!"

"That is impossible," Aal declared.

"Killing you would almost definitely be against the Virtue Code," Luiz said, twirling his hair.

"Perhaps you misheard," Robert chimed in.

"I did not mishear!" J. scowled at Robert. "It was very clear: 'Kill the beast! Cut his throat!'"

"'Kill the priest,' maybe?" Robert ventured. "'Gut his boat'?"

"Even so," Aal noted, "who's to say who 'the beast' is?"

"Perhaps they were looking for friend Sora," Luiz said, not even trying to conceal his glee.

"My dear," Aal turned to Luiz with the closest expression resembling disapproval she could muster, "I understand you have your concerns about friend Sora. But she is no 'beast.' That phrase is far more apt with respect to our visitor. If it were about him, I mean."

"It is probably a metaphor," Luiz accepted the reproach.

"Ah, indeed," Aal said. "Our students are very adept at meta-phor here. They consider literal truth to be so twentieth-century."

"It is almost definitely a metaphor," Luiz concurred with himself.

"Of course it's a metaphor!" J. shouted, breaking in. "A met-aphor for me!"

"No, you are more *like* a beast than an *actual* beast," Robert said. "A simile, more than a metaphor. I can sort of see why they might want to gut your boat."

J. glanced at him, confused. "I don't—"

"Friend J.," Aaliyah interrupted gently, worried by that look on his face. "Please, try to calm down."

"I am calm, Aal. This is me calm. I didn't do anything, Aal, and I don't understand why I am here."

There was a long silence.

"I'll get a lawyer," J. said into the silence.

"No, friend J., listen," Aaliyah answered quickly. "That will be seen as aggressive. You'll take a leave instead. Effective immediately."

"But I don't work here."

"Fair point," Aaliyah conceded, her voice softening. "Lis-ten, my dear. May I suggest that we all just take a deep breath? That we have some refreshment, some poco perhaps? Would and should do make you ill, drink a glass and it will pass?" She indi-cated the pitcher and compostable cups along the low shelf.

"What?" J. asked.

"Would and should do make you ill—"

"No, I mean what does that mean?"

"I don't understand, my dear."

"What?"

"What you are asking."

"I'm asking what that expression means."

"Isn't it just obvious what it means? I can't think of how to explain it without just repeating it."

"It is obvious," Luiz echoed.

"Our friend," Robert offered, retaking his cushion after having quickly helped himself to some poco, "has a lot on his mind. A lot going on. He is a currently a fugitive from virtue, after all. They may want to cut his throat, so we should cut him some slack."

"Robert," J. said, "I'm not entirely sure whose side you are on."

"Probably yours, friend," Robert sipped the poco.

"All I am saying, my dear," Aal did her best to explain, "is that we should continue talking. That we should just ride this little wrinkle out."

"Almost definitely let it pass," Luiz echoed.

"And what does that mean?" J. asked.

"To be perfectly frank, my dear, our students, God bless them, have a pretty short attention span. Within a few days they'll be angry about something else. They will forget entirely about this whole thing, which has nothing really to do with you at any rate."

"A few days? But—I am not staying here. I am leaving on the next ferry, whenever the hell that is. Speaking of which—"

"Of course you are free to leave at any time, my dear. But the President did ask me to convey our firm preference, our *firm* preference, that you remain among us until the wheels of virtue have completed their turn. Indeed Bob also asked that, while you remain among us, you please put on—where is it," Aal rummaged through some flap within her billowy gown, "Ah! Here it is!"

"The scarlet 'H'!" Robert exclaimed as the administrator proffered it to J., unable to conceal *his* glee.

"When is the next ferry out?" J. said as evenly as he could, feeling his face turning the color of the 'H.'

Aal sighed, withdrew the 'H.' "I believe that is 7:59, my dear. The last ferry of the night. I suppose if we wrap up in a moment …"

J. followed her glance to the clock on the wall, which read 7:36.

Just then the door swung open and Shawn, the student shadow, strode in feeling no need to apologize for his lateness. He glanced around the room, lingering on J. "I see that you have begun without me," he said without emotion.

"Just small talk," Aaliyah said, aware of this violation of the regulations.

"Nothing substantial," Luiz said to Shawn with a knowing

look. "How's it going, how do you do, that sort of thing."

"We were just explaining to our friend," Aaliyah continued, "that there is really nothing we can do, or should do, to stop anyone from expressing their feelings here. Freedom of feeling, and freedom to express feelings, are among our highest Community Values at Nevergreen, and the Virtue Code dictates that we uphold them at all costs. Like it or no, my dear, the Resistance has the right to speak."

"And the students would be upset at *any* effort to silence them as well," Luiz glanced knowingly at Shawn, who glanced knowingly back, then turned to his phone and began texting something.

"But this—that—is outrageous," J. almost whispered.

"Well, we support *your* free speech, too," Aal affirmed. "If that right belongs to you, then surely it belongs to them as well? Particularly," she looked meaningfully at him and dropped her voice, "given the controversial things you said."

"What? What was controversial?"

"It may not have been the words, per se. But your free speech created controversy."

"Therefore it was controversial," Luiz said.

"Can't you discourage them, at least? Use your own free speech to do that?" J. felt anger come on, feeling good that some anger was coming, he could almost hear Debra saying, you need to get angry sometimes, doc, you need to stop always *letting it slide.* "Their 'speech' is putting me in danger. That must be against your Virtue Code, no? Can't you charge them, or something? Threaten to? An Offensiveness Complaint against the students?"

"What?" Luiz responded with a start. "From a grown-up against a student? That doesn't even make sense."

"And on a practical level, my dear," Aaliyah added as if this were the most obvious thing in the world, "that would only inflame the situation. Make them angrier."

"Then can't you just discourage them—*somehow?* Ask them to refrain from judgment? Wait till the facts are in? Wait until

I've had a chance to defend myself?" J. paused. "I'll use my free speech. I'll defend myself."

"Oh no!" Aal and Luiz exclaimed.

"No, no, no," Aal added firmly, "you mustn't do that, my dear."

"Defend myself?"

"Absolutely not. You'll just get *everyone* angrier at you. As if you're blaming them for being offended by you."

"Just stay silent," Luiz said. "Let us handle it for you."

"But you've just said—you can't stop them. You can't even discourage them."

"Exactly," Aal said.

"We'll ignore them," Luiz added.

"Yes," Aal agreed. "That is precisely what we will do. Nothing."

What happened next was a blur. The door swung open again, an entire mob of shouting students swarmed in no doubt summoned by that weasel shadow Shawn, and J., never having any idea he was capable of any such thing, had, in the blur, what was the word—*defenestration*, that was it, he remembered it from that novel about the murdered philosopher, Descartes, defenestration was the act that started that long seventeenth-century war; funny what you think of when you're in the middle of a life-threatening crisis—never having any idea he was capable of any such thing, J. had defenestrated himself out the third floor window.

23

HE WAS RUNNING, AWAY from the Hex, down a hill, in the moonlight, through some brush, the branches scratching, his arm, his face, his torso, he was Wound Man, impaled, impaled again. He was running down the hill but he was slowing down, out of breath, on the path, following the stones, he accidentally kicked a couple as he ran that rolled down the hill with him. That marsh was to his right, the sanctuary somewhere to the left. The guesthouse would be ahead, the abandoned guesthouse. He'd never had his morning coffee, his three cups sometimes four, usually four, he and Debra had their shared vice, too much coffee lately maybe, she had been talking about their health, thinking about their health, maybe less coffee, better nutrition, maybe exercise. You know the boys are getting older, she said, they're more independent, there was more time for them, the two of them, to start, you know, being a couple again, if he wanted to. She didn't say exactly that but that is what she meant, he thought, she said weren't there better ways to spend your midlife crisis than so focused on those paintings, the diseases, the surgeries, to be honest he was starting to become a little dark, dark like his coffee which he liked with a single drop of cream, three or four or five cups of which he most definitely had not drunk this morning. Funny what you think about when you are running for your life, he thought again, not running, he had slowed to walk, still breathing heavily, then made himself continue.

That was pretty slick, that maneuver in the tree. Good thing that tree was right outside the window because otherwise what, exactly, was he thinking—*defenestrating*—himself that way? In a way it was thrilling, he had to admit. The spontaneity, the adrenaline pumping even without the caffeine in his veins, for a moment he couldn't remember, had he actually opened the window or had he just crashed through it? A second wind, the guesthouse was to his right so he bore left on the path, following the stones, picked up his step, in a few moments he would be on the damn boat and on his damn way out of here. He'd have to figure out how to get back to the airport of course but after defenestrating himself and shimmering down the tangled branches of that tree with a horde of hate-hating maniacs on his tail how hard could it be to find a ride to an airport in the civilized world? Running full speed again, it was almost eight, he still had a few minutes, he was sure, he recognized the path ahead lit by the moon and the stones, the stones, he had run the right way, the right direction, any journey with you Debra is by definition the right direction, he remembered saying that, he put it in the book, she said how can you know, I mean really *know*, and he said you can know because I am not him, Debra, it is *me* he said squeezing her hand and not letting go, all the way down, and she said that was the moment that she knew … and now the right direction was this one, just round this bend, back to the world, back to Debra, really this was going to be a terrific story when he got home, he was already thinking about how to embellish it a little, play up the drama, he did always sort of want to be a writer—

As he rounded the bend his heart lifted as he saw the brightly illuminated dock, the many white lights strung along it, the inviting waiting area, sheltered, heated, they were of course running the heaters in the late autumn chill, he saw the light over the post on which was mounted the plastic display of tourist brochures with a little sign over it saying *Welcome to Nevergreen*, and he saw the lights on the rear of the ferry that had departed with its last group of day-trippers some three minutes early and was now making its way back to the civilized world, and to Debra, without him.

The last ferry of the night.

J. stood there breathing heavily, breathing loudly, making cloudy puffs in the night air. He stared at the lights of the boat until they disappeared into the dark swirling waters. For some reason he looked up, toward the night sky, and saw that, directly above him, on a silky thread hanging from the branch above, a squishy caterpillar was slowly descending without a care in the world. Strangely this didn't bother him as he stood, he watched, he envied this carefree creature, he was so absorbed in watching the slow patient descent of this simple little animal that he did not hear the clamor of footsteps coming up the path behind him. This was one, of several, reasons he was so surprised when he heard someone calling behind him, when he turned around to see a band of Confederate soldiers aiming their Pattern 1861 Enfield short-barreled musketoons at him, and firing.

24

"Fuck, this thing is uncomfortable," the Second Lieutenant (for so he liked to think of himself) had said as he wiggled around, his bare skin itching literally *everywhere* under the low-quality imitation wool fabric.

"Yah," concurred the Third Lieutenant (who did not think of himself this way, despite ranking as such), also perspiring despite the crisp air. "Fucking hot, too."

"Jeebus, ladies, will you man up already?" the Colonel of Truth muttered for perhaps the fifth time this afternoon, thinking, also for the fifth time, that it was time to find better lackeys. Speaking of which, where the hell had Spencer disappeared to anyway?

"You think the real uniforms were this uncomfortable?" the Second Lieutenant asked a few minutes later. They had learned after their encounter with the harpies and Queen Bee Sora—he felt kind of bad watching the woman shrink away instead of obeying the call to the gathering—that the uniforms were Confederate but also knock-offs. The latter was a bummer, but more than compensated for by the coolness of the former.

"Maybe that's why they lost," the fourth-ranked lackey suggested. He rarely spoke, and the others weren't even sure of his name, but he did always bring the beer.

"Damn, man, maybe we would have still had slavery today if they'd had better uniforms," the Second Lieutenant snickered, accepting high fives all around. The Lieutenant had joined the Colonel at the urging of his Neo-Nazi clubmates, who were hoping to create solidarity coalitions with what they thought were similar-minded groups; originally resistant he was finally convinced when that chick Ariana, elected *Führer* of the club on the coalition platform, offered to blow him too. What a great semester he was having, really: getting head from the head, headbanging with his Neo-Nazi pals and banging the heads of those Ur-Nazi asswipes, all while throwing himself headlong into his Dishonors Thesis and Practicum—arguing, in the fall, for the de-lionization of Martin Luther King, Jr. and then, in the spring, leading the march on Washington, D.C., to tear down the monument there.

The Colonel sighed, tiring of his lackeys' racist shit. "Look, you ignorani. These were the best I could find on Amazon, in our budgets. And at least we also got the muskets." He did not mention that he'd also thought the rifles were real when Amazon recommended them. Well, at least they were real*istic*, and the loud air-gun *pop* they made was really startling. "Do you need to drill disassembling and reassembling one more time?"

"Nah, nah, we're good, Colonel," the Second Lieutenant said. He was quite happy that Spencer had disappeared; he could almost *taste* First Lieutenant now. "Should we go ahead and do the selfie? These fuckers are uncomfortable, but they are mad cool."

"We'll wait for Spencer," the Colonel declared in that bossy way of his.

"So what's the plan again?" the Third Lieutenant said, revealing again why he was ranked only third.

The Colonel sighed. After the grueling afternoon he really wished he could find better lieutenants. He did have two other students in training, but they had proved their worthlessness first by refusing to buy the uniforms and then by going (against orders!) to the gathering. Well, at least there was success on one front, inspired, he was sure, by his own example and his useless lackeys: by late afternoon he had seen several dozen students also flouting that latest fascist student council resolution. By tonight perhaps they'd have a critical mass and this place would really understand what it meant to "Keep It Crazy."

"Okay, listen carefully, ladies," the Colonel said, "because I don't want to have to say any of this again. This afternoon saw this place descend truly into the realm of the ignorant and the asinine. That Teach-In was a veritable orgy of ignoranosity. The only thing more ignoraneous than that was the gathering. Now am I right?"

"But we didn't go to the gathering," the Third Lieutenant said, very aware of the Colonel's use of the word *orgy*.

"We didn't have to, to know that it was filled with ignoraneity. That is what we are fighting here. That is why we have uniforms. To stand up for, to fight for, the Truth." The Colonel thought of the many honorable men who had died in uniform in defense of Truth. "In this dark age, in this dark place, the solemn duty has fallen to us to honor the Truth around here, to seek the Truth around here, should it somehow appear. We Shoot for the Truth." Ooh, good one, he thought. "And so we must honor all those who attempt to speak the Truth. Am I right, ladies?"

"What does that mean, exactly?" the Second Lieutenant hesitated, again raising the question of how he had earned this high a rank.

"The guy last night," the fourth lackey said quietly, who lately, with his supply of beer, was definitely ascending the ranks.

"Exactly," the Colonel lifted his fake musket.

"We're going to shoot him?" the Third Lieutenant asked.

Both the Colonel and the fourth lackey sighed. The Third Lieutenant glared at the latter suspiciously, not at all liking what he was seeing lately.

"No," the Colonel said in resignation. "We shall raise our Muskets of Truth in his honor. And then—"

"Shoot him?" the Second Lieutenant was trying to follow.

"These aren't real, you ignoranus!" the Colonel exclaimed.

"You ignoranus!" the Third Lieutenant echoed, slapping the Second Lieutenant's face and glaring at the fourth lackey, making sure he saw.

"Forget it," the Colonel was beyond irritation. "Just straighten your uniforms, ladies, and let's go Shoot for Truth!"

So off they went into the night, this band of brothers, this confederacy of dunces, led by this not-an-idiot-savant-but-just-plain-idiot, in search of a man they had arbitrarily decided was the perfect symbol of whatever it was they thought worthy of honoring. Since they were without an actual plan, they were surely quite lucky to happen to be passing the Center for Community Priorities in Hexant 4 when the man himself came dropping, falling, crashing down through the tree, crashed onto the ground, then stood himself up and set off running.

"That's him," the fourth lackey whispered, the only one of them to have been monitoring the *Howler*'s website that day to keep on top of the news, and thus in a position to identify the man.

"That's him," the Second Lieutenant echoed more loudly, hoping the Colonel hadn't heard the fourth lackey's whisper.

So off they set in pursuit, following the man down the hill, onto the path, past the guidestones onto the trail. He was heading toward the ferry but he was fast, or faster than they at any rate, not encumbered as they were by these heavy, overheating uniforms and cumbersome musketoons. He disappeared ahead of them briefly but they forged on, they followed the path, and moments later they came out in the dock area. They saw him standing there looking up at the sky, or into the tree, was he admiring creation, was he petitioning, or praying, or maybe weeping, it didn't matter as they assembled into the formation they had been drilling, with some spontaneous readjustment given the unaccounted for absence of the First Lieutenant.

"Ladies," the Colonel said solemnly as they steadied, "before us in the moonlight is a man unafraid to speak Truth to Power, and to the Powerless. It is our duty, and our time, to honor this man." He called out loudly, "Sir? Sir?"

The four of them, maybe ten yards off, stood stiffly, raised their muskets and stuck barrels firmly against shoulders, pointed squarely at the man as he turned around, then put their fingers on the triggers and applied some gentle pressure.

"Esteemed Shooter of Bullets of Truth," the Colonel honestly felt that he had never been more alive, "we return your fire."

More or less simultaneously the band of brothers began pulling their triggers.

25

"Jesus Christ!" J. screamed when he heard the *pop* sounds, simply not believing what his eyes were telling him, that he was being shot at. *Drop and roll* popped into his head, God knows where from, it was that time he and Debra were stuck at that meeting with the whole goddamn team of teachers, that interminable meeting where they were hearing about the many challenges facing and presented by you know who, *again*, and she had mouthed those words at him across the table nodding toward the exit and it was all they could do to suppress their laughter, the release of all that pent-up tension, the impossibility of *their* challenge, well drop and roll J. did, twisting his body with surprising agility as he rolled to his right under the bushes near the dock.

He paused under the bushes. The soldiers had come up the path after him but now seemed to be arguing among themselves rather than pursuing him. That didn't make a lot of sense but it also didn't seem wise to stick around trying to make sense of it. He began crawling through the bushes, the underbrush. More scratches, maybe a bruise or two, but he didn't feel them, didn't feel the chill, didn't reflect on how odd it was that he, a respected medical professional, was crawling through overgrown woods at night, but kept crawling. A few minutes later he came out onto something like a path, no guidestones here but a path anyway, under the rising full moon. He paused again, to catch his breath, and bearings.

Way, way off he heard murmurings, shouting, clamoring. But in the vicinity was only wilderness, the whisperings of the woods at night, some crickets, insects, nocturnal mammals maybe. And to his right, not far, the lapping waters of the bay.

"This way," someone whispered, but then he realized it was himself whispering aloud. Odd thing to whisper because there really was only one way, stretching in front of him. J. took that first step and stepped into something squishy under his foot. *Finally*, he thought, in need of some of that pig-shit good luck. Instead, he saw in the moonlight as he scraped the mess from his shoe, it was what remained of a couple of caterpillars.

Doesn't matter, J. thought as a branch snapped nearby and he took off ahead.

After a while he came to a spot where the path split into a fork. The left fork seemed to lead deeper into woods, which, by his recollection of the map crumpled in his jacket pocket, were probably the outer reaches of the sanctuary. That fact, and the fact that he remembered the fork on the drive to Nevergreen— he'd gone left there and look how *that* turned out—made it easy to choose the right fork here, which should keep him on the periphery of the island and away from the madness in the center. All ways lead to the madness, he thought as he walked, remembering that strange driver's remark; a thought confirmed a short while later, after the path curved slightly inland and then came to a branching point with a half-dozen paths leading away, at the intersection of which was one of those destination signs with many different arrows. As J. could see in the clear moonlight, each indicated that the asylum was "this way."

J. sighed, contemplated, deliberated.

He was about to pull the map from his pocket when there was a scampering in the brush, a nocturnal mammal, he thought, perhaps some piglets, or maybe Confederate soldiers. He plunged down a path to his right, trying to remember the map, the rough geometry. This section of the island, down near the water, was outside and probably passing the limits of the sanctuary. There was a path on the map, the Footpath it was called, he remembered that, and he recalled that it was connected to a beach, a beach with some funny name. He wasn't sure what he was hoping for but if the path he was on might lead to the Footpath, and the Footpath was connected to a beach, then there would be water; if there were water, there might be boats; and if there were boats, perhaps he could find some other way off this island before the next goddamn ferry that was only scheduled to depart tomorrow morning, Aal had said.

"I could be dead by then," he had moaned to Robert during the meeting with the administrators, right before the mob stormed in.

"Nah," Robert dissented, "badly wounded, tops."

J. slowed down, caught his breath, followed the path. It began descending and soon he came upon the beach. He paused, pulled the map from his pocket. The clouds beginning to fill the sky only partially obscured the moon, leaving enough light to confirm that the Footpath he had entered was the first stretch of the beach, and to remind him that the beach was named Icke Beach, after the early benefactor who had donated his sociopathic twins to the asylum's infamous early twins studies. J. looked up at the clouds, then out at the water. Far off, across the shimmering darkness, were twinkling lights, civilization. But to get there he needed a boat, and someone who knew how to drive a boat. As he set off down the beach, along the Footpath, he remembered that story Debra had told him about her parents. He had put it in the book, their adventure with the sailboat that had ended so dramatically, engendering all those "what ifs," those regrets, that resentment. It was getting darker now with the thickening clouds and the dark water all around but the rustling of the waves, the loud swirling of water, was soothing, like a noise machine. He supposed, if necessary, he could spend the night here, on this beach. He was cold, he realized, calming down now, in this too-thin jacket, and the sharp breeze off the water was not helping. But a little cold he could handle, he thought, as he stepped through the sand and stepped again onto something squishy. Whatever it was, caterpillar, pig-droppings, he barely flinched, it didn't matter given the bigger matters he was grappling with. But the same was not true a few moments later when, stepping over some rocks, he stepped onto something rubbery and hard and covered with something sticky, stumbled, and then fell onto something else equally rubbery and hard and sticky.

The cold he could handle. Less so the fact that what he had stumbled on, and on to, were a pair of dismembered human feet.

That's when he heard the bloodcurdling scream, at the same moment as his own.

26

MAHLIA AND JENNA EMERGED from the Footpath convulsing in giggles. They had been waiting in the bushes for nearly twenty minutes after finishing their installation and couldn't believe their luck in getting to observe their first victim.

"A thing of beauty," Mahlia giggled, her hand on her chest.

"A thing of beauty," Jenna mimicked Mahlia's gesture by putting her hand on Mahlia's chest as well, and using her other hand to take the selfie of them. "Say cheese!"

"Cheese! That scream you did," Mahlia said, not removing Jenna's hand.

"Totally spontaneous, babe."

"Perfect. Sounded like—"

"Someone having his foot cut off?"

"Ha! I really have to hand it to you."

They both giggled at this. Jenna, looking around as they entered the path back up from the beach, seeing no one, moved her hand down toward Mahlia's crotch. "Maybe," she whispered, "you could hand me this?"

"Mmm," Mahlia moaned, removing Jenna's hand from her crotch, but holding it. "Later, babe. After the party. We have to go get dressed. *Then* undressed."

"I could skip the FOMO," Jenna squeezed Mahlia's hand, referring to the campus "Foam and Pomo Party" scheduled, at the Intersections Lounge, after the Moondial ceremony.

"After all the work we did?" Their matching outfits, the giant labia majora and labia minora they were planning to debut that night, had taken hours of hard, but loving, labor. "Patience, babe. Now hey. Do you think—he'll be okay?" She nodded toward the beach.

"I don't know. He looked pretty terrified."

"What if he, you know, like has a heart attack down there? This could really backfire."

"I don't know, babe," Jenna said. "It's, like, performance art."

"Can murder be performance art, babe?" Mahlia fretted.

"Maybe. Maybe. But that would totally beat Zoro by a mile." Zoro was the undisputed performance art champion on campus, as master of vomiting on demand. So far this year he had already thrown up at convocation, the allegiance ceremony for the Virtue Code, and of course at the gathering earlier. Word was that he had something *major* planned for the Moondial.

Now that they were thinking about it, though, the guy did look pretty old, the way he shuffled along the beach in that little old guy jacket. Jenna's scream had been perfectly timed, coinciding with the guy's own scream when he realized that the black clumps just visible along the beach were apparently dismembered feet.

"It was pretty funny though," Mahlia conceded. "The way he collapsed on the sand."

"That girlish scream."

"The way he clutched his heart."

"He *was* a pretty old guy."

They both hesitated.

"I mean, he did get up, babe," Jenna offered.

"Yeah, but ran the wrong way, babe," Mahlia fretted again.

"He'll eventually turn around."

"There's like snakes down there."

"He *was* like totally clutching his heart."

"This could like *really* backfire, babe."

They both hesitated again.

"You're totally right, babe," Jenna squeezed Mahlia's hand. "Like, a real catastrophe."

"But it was unintended."

"It was an honest mistake, babe."

"Bad judgment, that's all. We've been vaping too much."

"Definitely, babe. We've been working so hard."

"So hard."

"Too hard."

"*Way* too hard."

"We needed to cut loose."

"Anybody would."

"We feel, like, terrible, babe. We have to take a selfie." They squeezed together, looked glum as Jenna snapped the photo and uploaded it to her Instagram. Several smileys and V's for virtue emoticons instantly appeared.

"Babe, this time we really," Mahlia said, already feeling a little better from the positive feedback and a lot better from their squeezing together, "like put our foot in our mouth."

Jenna felt better too, feeling, well, *stirrings*. "Let's get out of here, babe. You know—like, one foot in front of the other."

Mahlia giggled, and pointed down. "I'm very attached to my feet."

"You can't," Jenna pulled Mahlia's hand to lead her back up the path toward campus, "let people walk all over you."

"You know, babe, if he does kick the bucket," Mahlia said, her own stirrings suggesting that now was perhaps "later" enough, "he'll end up like six feet under. Fuck the FOMO, babe. I've got some pomo back in my room."

"We can just use our own," Jenna breathed, "majora and minora."

"You, babe," Mahlia brushed Jenna's breasts with her one hand while she now pulled *her* up the path with her other, "are about to get extremely laid."

"Watch the fuck you're going!" Some large male students coming down to enter the Footpath nearly collided in the dark with Mahlia and Jenna and, being way too messed up to realize how hot was the scene before them, reacted angrily. The girls were themselves too preoccupied with the extraordinary sexual activity coming their way to notice that these other students, one of whom had actually spent last week designing costumes with Jenna for the theater department, were dressed up frighteningly realistically as zombies—at least insofar as zombies could be realistic.

"Fuck, Deck, asshole, you were supposed to bring the cooler," Gever said as they got down to the Footpath, insisting his roommate was designated to bring along the blood-red cocktail they had mixed earlier in the lodge. Gever was the sort who would have been on a rugby team had he gotten in to any college other than Nevergreen, so you probably didn't want to get him upset at you, generally speaking. As it was, his application to Nevergreen had been very much buoyed by the renovated (and now eponymed) gym his family had included with his application fee.

Spending most of his time at that gym was Decker, who himself would have been an offensive lineman on a football team if he had gotten in to any college other than Nevergreen. "Fuck you, asshole, I'm *way* too wasted to remember any fucking coolers," he answered using the word *asshole* as a term of endearment, having just popped another DMT tablet and thinking it might be nice to snuggle a little with that seaweed along the shore.

"Fuck you both, you assholes, it's no fucking big deal," said Benno also using it as an endearment, pulling up the rear. As he said this he flexed his gym-enhanced biceps and shifted the awesome heavy axe he was carrying to his other shoulder, then adjusted his awesome new little round glasses on his straight nose. Having just popped *two* DMT tablets he was filled with nothing but love for all the wonderful things that were going to happen tonight.

"Fuck, probably the vampires have it, those fuckwads," Gever perseverated, referring to those probably gay fuckwads downstairs from them who referred to themselves as the Princes of Darkness. "They were asking a lot of fucking questions about it." Indeed they had, when they were selling Gever the DMT the three of them had been popping since the gathering.

"Gev, let it the fuck go, asshole," Benno said affectionally.

"I got the brains. I got the fucking stove. We look fucking awesome. We don't need the fucking blood."

They *did* look fucking awesome, Benno thought, though it had gotten dark with the moon nearly fully obscured by the clouds. They had taken some bad-ass selfies in the lodge before setting out. The torn clothes were cake; but the zombie makeup job, that was pretty fucking awesome, if he did say so himself, thinking that if he hadn't gotten in to Nevergreen he would probably already be pursuing his dream of being a professional costume designer.

"Fine, asshole," Gever said. "So give me the fucking brains and the stove. Let's set up right here. Deck, what the fuck you doing?"

"It's so beautiful," Decker said, sitting by the water, stroking the seaweed.

"I'll do it, boss." Benno pulled from his backpack the thermos with the sausage and liver concoction he had prepared in the lodge kitchen that afternoon, using Ezequiell's recipe, and set up the stove to warm it up. He had tried to convince the man to join them this evening, because what could be better than zombies down at the beach, munching some hot brains and guzzling some cold blood (if it hadn't been forgotten), and maybe howling a little at the full moon? Okay, the full moon was now hidden behind clouds, and the howling was a werewolf thing, but then who wouldn't, with a belly full of brains and blood, want to do some moon-howling anyway? Ezequiell had declined, alas, wanting to pursue the piglet hunt through the evening, leaving Benno stuck with these two assholes. But hey, it was all good, glorious even. They would just meet up at the FOMO-fest later and then *really* get that party started.

"Fucking check me out, assholes," Gever said, popping another DMT. He had smeared some of the meat mixture around his mouth, extended his arms zombie-style, and was stumbling spastically, moaning, "Brains! Brains!" He cracked up in that clogged-sinus, snorting way of his. "Join me, asshole. That asshole over there has checked out."

He pointed over to Decker, who was lying on the sand slowly humping the seaweed. Benno suddenly had the inspiration that seaweed was really an underutilized resource, making a mental note to remember this when he was pursuing his other dream, of being a flower arranger. Why the fuck not, he thought. "Must ... Eat ... Brains!" he moaned, arms extended zombie-style, stumbling spastically beside his roommate.

They had barely lurched three steps along the Footpath when they were nearly run over by a man running back up the Footpath at full speed, screaming like a little girl.

"Watch the fuck you're going!" both Gever and Benno shouted after the figure, who didn't slow down to respond.

A moment later came the first rumbles of thunder.

27

THERE WERE FIVE WINDOWS, four of which were boarded up and the last with broken panes. The front door was secured by planks loosely nailed over it, some on top of others, suggesting there had been repeated reinforcement. The side door was either locked or just stuck. But the rear door, fortunately, had a couple of small panes of intact glass, one of which ended its six-year run of intactness when J. rammed his fist through to reach down and unlock the door. Never mind the shards, the cuts, the dripping blood, these were just a few more wounds accumulated this evening. The door was still stuck, he had to push, he pushed again, and it gave way. It was pitch-dark but he could tell, from intuition, that the place was a dump—*a shithole* came to mind—okay it wasn't intuition but from the dankness and the stench and the silky cobwebs that snared his face as he pushed inside. The roof was also leaking in several spots, but, he thought, it would do while he waited out both the downpour and his cardiac dysrhythmia. From the look of things and the feel of things (the thrumping), this was going to be a while.

And why shouldn't it be? He was still in shock from the feet on the beach, that bloodcurdling scream. That long run stumbling over more detached feet on the beach, stumbling into that thicket of weeds, feeling *something* slithering beneath his own feet, then coming up to that—that *cliff*, why shouldn't there be a cliff here, it was a steep hill to the upper campus, there was elevation, and on the beach it was a dead end. He'd turned around, gone back through the field of feet, but the rest was a haze, except he was under the impression that he had nearly collided with a gang of zombies as he was fleeing the beach and he also had images of himself climbing an extremely steep hill on his hands and knees to get himself up here to this building, which, he thought, was on the periphery of the upper campus.

He crouched in the middle of the room, away from the steady drips from the ceiling, as his heartbeat returned to normal. It smelled damp in here, not just the current rain but ongoing, moldy. Maybe even something vaguely rotten. And—what was that, some other absolutely disgusting smell. It was utterly dark. The lightbulbs that hadn't been shattered had long ago burned out; and anyway with that first blast of lightning the power had gone out on the whole island. This J. had determined immediately on breaking into the place because he had finally broken down and tried to call his wife, only to learn that with the cable out, the entire island was in the dead zone. When he had managed to stop jabbing the useless phone buttons, when he had managed to choke down the tears welling up, he had found this relatively dry spot in the middle of the room and crouched—to wait out the storm, the power outage, his time in this place, his life.

Feeling calmer he pulled out his phone again and switched on the flashlight. In the dim glow he could see why the place smelled moldy: there was actual mold in patches on the wall. The house *was* filthy, cobwebs everywhere, with trays and paper plates half-filled with long decayed food, hard moldy bagels maybe, spreads turned green and solidified, dried up half-consumed fish. *Petrified* came to mind, in both its senses, like archeologists opening an ancient tomb and discovering that some festive party had been interrupted here, abandoned, years and years before—there was overturned smashed furniture, there were remnants of small fires in two of the corners now soaked from the leaking roof, and—he got up from his spot and went over to inspect—were those old smears of dried blood splattered on the wall? Almost certainly, he thought with revulsion, also noticing (with more revulsion) that two or three caterpillars were ascending the wall amidst the splatters.

J. shuddered, retreated to the dry spot in the center. Whatever this place was, something dreadful had happened here.

Oh, and he also determined the source of the disgusting smell. As he resumed his position in the center he noticed two piles of fresh pig-droppings just a foot away from him. With a stench like that, he thought, those pigs had to be carnivorous, Brenda's "you have a wonderful imagination" notwithstanding.

Well it can't hurt, he thought. He got up and stepped squarely in one of the piles. It was disgusting, but ultimately, he thought, necessary. Kind of like life. Oh, good one, he thought without much enthusiasm, realizing—as he resumed his crouch in the dark, in the filth, surrounded by these smells, his hand hurting from its most recent wounds, listening to the rain hammering the roof and dripping in through the leaks—that he was again really, really hungry.

He tried his phone again; cable still dead.

He was remembering that restaurant, that café downtown, Cozzens, closed a few years back but they used to go every New Year's Day for breakfast to commemorate—no, it wasn't their first date, it was their second—or at least they did until the monsters started arriving and everything began to change. He remembered looking at her that first January first morning, she was sad-eyed and tired but oh so beautiful, he knew already in that moment that they would return to that restaurant every New Year's Day forever, drinking that fantastic coffee and those omelettes—those omelettes, he could almost taste them—he didn't know at that time what a fantastic cook Debra was, but what he did know was that he would be eating those omelettes with her every New Year's Day for the rest of their lives. All right well the place closed down a few years back but still—

He was thinking about this when several things happened at the same time.

There was another great flash of lightning and this time instantaneous earth-shattering thunder that sounded (he would have thought, had he time to think) like the opening salvo of Armageddon.

Somewhere in the sanctuary Zeke's carnivores, their face and body paint streaked on their half-naked bodies from crawling through the rain, had done what nobody, not even they, believed, they could do: not merely sighted some piglets but managed to isolate one from the drove, corner it, and they were at this moment in the pouring rain advancing upon it, spears in hand and lust for blood in their hearts, as the terrified little animal began squealing its heart out and emptying its bowels all over the place.

And at the same moment J. heard the rattling of the front, side, and rear doors, loose planks being ripped off, doors being forced and crashing open, and the room suddenly being invaded from every direction (he would reflect afterward because it was too fast in the moment) with goddamn screaming Nazis and could those be screaming Islamic terrorists, was that German he was hearing and *Allāhu akbar* screams as they tore through the webs of caterpillar silk, taking selfies as they invaded? It was all so fast there was hardly time to notice that there were two different Nazi uniforms, the Neo-Nazis and the Ur-Nazis who bickered about everything bickered also about their dress, nor was there time to notice the different patterns on the keffiyeh-masks worn by the Jihadis because the club members with different geographical and national and religious allegiances also bickered about everything including their dress, and certainly they all bickered with the Neo- and Ur-Nazis who bickered with them, and there were others, were they wearing red shirts, shouting "Hate hate! Hate hate!" who bickered with all of them, they all bickered about everything, except for the one thing they agreed on, which was about the anniversary of The Episode, which they mutually commemorated with an annual good old-fashioned re-thrashing of this now abandoned house. J. had not had time to notice any of this, of course, because as fast as you can say lickety-split (he thought afterward, when there *was* time to say lickety-split), he had defenestrated himself for the second time in his life, and that evening.

28

J. SCREAMED AS A thousand shards of glass flew in every direction—some, he was sure, into his eyeballs.

All right, his eyes were actually closed and maybe it was only the sharp raindrops crashing against his eyelids as he burst back outside and started running. Without any intended direction, for having a direction would have been pointless given that he hadn't formulated any plan as to where to go—other than off this goddamn island, if only that were even possible.

He had jumped through many hoops in his career and life, it was true. There was medical school, residency, fellowships; the private practice, the return to the hospital; getting Debra to move in with him, that was some work, then to marry him, that was more work; dealing with the challenges of having so ridiculously many children (for so three seemed to him, but it didn't take much bantering with Debra to realize that that was what she *really* wanted). But he was too busy running through woods, through cold rain and snow—okay, no snow, and perhaps the rain had stopped—to marvel over the fact that he had spent the evening jumping not through hoops but windows. Later— should he survive to tell the tale—he would surely regale Debra and the monsters, how he had dived through those windows, the thousand shards of glass—all right maybe the first window was actually open and the second he had managed to open before diving—well anyway he had spent the evening escaping from maniacs, Nazis, and terrorists, what exactly had *they* been doing all night?

The rain *was* over, he noticed with relief as he came out from the trees and approached the Hex from behind one of the Pacman buildings. The damage had been done: there was mud, downed branches, mini-floods, and, he could see from the darkened buildings, still no power. But the moon was back out and on its way to the meridian, and with it hope was on the ascent as well. Just—he checked his phone, noticed the battery was starting to get low—eight-plus hours until the ferry.

He paused outside the Hex, taking it in in the charged glow of the full moon, seeing the outer hedges of the Maze, the ramps beneath leading down into the Crypt. Whole place seemed serene now, the rain had cleared everyone out. There was a student lodge to his left, also dark, quiet. Where was everybody, he wondered. It was peaceful, really, he almost didn't mind when he picked up one of the sodden mushes of posterboard discarded on the ground, saw that it was a mask of—well of him, of that photo that awful girl had taken. Dreadful likeness, really. He stared at the wet mask, in the moonlight, the sinister shadows. He looked so—old—he thought, tired, worn out. When had that happened? Jesus what an evening, it really couldn't get any worse. Though of course with still eight hours ahead who knows what this place might cook up.

But now what to do?

He looked again at the mask.

He looked at the empty Hex, the Maze in the middle. So open, exposed, vulnerable, he thought. He really wouldn't mind some sleep, he was worn out, tired to the core. The guesthouse, abandoned, no thank you. The student lodge, also dark, apparently empty, he suddenly recalled the brochure's description of the Crypt, imagined all the students mummified in their beds, still wearing their hoodies, *way* too creepy, no thank you. Find a couch in some building, one of these darkened Pacmans? The nearest one was this Pacman here, in Hexant 2. Home to philosophy and religion, other humanities, classics too before that went belly-up. The Socratic Center for the Non-Pursuit of Wisdom it was called, because (the brochure explained) Socrates famously taught, via his method of *elenchus* or "refutation," that he is wisest who knows he knows nothing. It seemed to follow, then, that he who knows least, knows most. There can't be much going on in *that* building, J. thought, making it a good place for a snooze.

J. maneuvered around the rear of the building, sticking close to its wall, feeling safer in back rather than in the open Hex. Thus it was that he soon found himself by the entrance to the— well it was hard to read the sign in the moonshadow created by the awning, though it did occur to him that if he had lost his eyes from the shards of glass it would have been even harder to read it—he peered more closely and could make out the words, "The Jakobus de Bedlem Museum of Curiosities."

Who had mentioned the museum. Brenda, at the beginning, right. Told the history of this place, said the brochure. The conditions of nineteenth-century mental asylums, the methods of treatment, the modes of restraint, the exorcisms, secret dungeons, crawl spaces. The tunnels, some system of tunnels had allegedly been built but later never found. Some story about the namesake, a Dutch missionary who had visions on a visit to the Holy Land, or was it that the benefactor of the Museum was some descendent of such? There were two display windows at the entrance and in the shadow he could just make out, in the first window, a mannequin with—must have been hundreds of needles sticking out of it. J. remembered from one of his history of medicine books the late nineteenth-century heyday of needle therapy for mental illness, an offshoot of the acupuncture recently immigrated with the Chinese. The western psychiatric twist was the placement of these needles primarily in the anus, urethra, and the eyeballs. J. was glad that, in the dark, he was unable to make out what was in the second display window.

That's when the power snapped back on.

It wasn't just that lights came back all over campus, that the Pacmans were all speckled in light. You could almost feel the power, the buzz and hum (J. imagined) of an electric chair frying its convict, the buzz and hum of an orchestra of electric lights. *Let there be light*, he thought, feeling the relief of the return, the cable, the mainland, the possibility of—calling his wife. He reached for his phone but then noticed that now, illuminated, he could see, first, the several caterpillars crawling up the glass of the second display window.

But then he could see the contents of that window.

There was a large posterboard displaying the cover of that final book by Dr. Taslitz M. Fester, *Humour and Pus*. The cover illustration was one that even J., with his obsession with wounds and dissection and cadavers, instantly regretted he could never unsee, and which shall remain undescribed here. He stood, and stared, immobile, not bothering to read the adjacent posterboard explaining the timing of the exhibit, that Grand Island was anticipating this very fall, perhaps this very week, perhaps this very night, the next installment of the ninety-nine-year cycle of a highly invasive caterpillar that had devastated the place almost a century before. Never mind the ecological damage back then, the inmates, already insane, only went more so at finding the disgusting squishy things in their meals, their clothes, their beds, their hair, and the occasional orifice. It was to deal with this invasion that the authorities had introduced the deadly *Cordyceps sinensis* fungus to the island, and it was then to deal with the invasive spread of that fungus that they had introduced the sometimes carnivorous piglets who so loved to munch on that fungus as well as the mummified carcasses of the caterpillars and who now left their droppings all over the island.

But J. was not learning about all this, nor remembering from the Clubs Expo that the school had a secret society also named "Humour and Pus" and thus not wondering about its connection to Fester's work. Nor (happily) was he aware of the two or three caterpillars that were, that very moment, descending from the awning on their threads directly toward the crown of his head. No he was not aware of any of these things because he was frozen, staring at the subtitle to Fester's book.

The Secret History of Ignoratio P. Elenchi's *Erucarium Ortus*, or, *The Wondrous Transformation of Caterpillars*.

J. stood, and stared, his heart pounding.

Was this about him? Was it about Debra? Was her goddamn father coming back from the grave—

He started running.

Again.

29

He always had this dream, different variations, same idea. Debra, formerly a research psychologist and now a clinical psychologist, had studied dreams extensively and believed they were meaningless. He believed that she was wrong and liked to tell her this, particularly when they were bantering. Consider his favorite awful recurring dream, something like this. He is running, comes to a door, a locked door. He somehow breaks the lock, closes the door behind him, is feeling around the wall to find the light when the light instead finds him. A bright flashlight, a spotlight, blinding him. Turn that off! he demands into the darkness. The reply is a sudden, sharp report, a bullet smashing into the wall just behind his left ear.

Hey! he exclaims.

Missed, a deep voice mutters from beyond the beam.

What!

I was aiming for your right ear, Q.

Are you out of your mind! he exclaims. You could have killed me.

I know, the voice says, as another shot rings out and smashes into the wall just behind his right ear.

Hey! he exclaims again.

Missed again, the voice says. I was aiming for your left ear, Q.

You're crazy! J. screams, squinting into the light.

I know, Q, the voice says.

And why are calling me Q? J.'s heart pounds.

It's only logical, the voice says, nonsense dressed up as sense.

J. feels the onset of panic. What do you want from me? he tries to breathe.

What, the voice says from the darkness, is the product of three times three, Q?

What?

The square of three, please. You have the count of five to tell me what I want to hear or I shall be forced to shoot again. One, two—

All right, all right. It's nine!

Another shot rings out, shattering J.'s right hand. He screams, falls to his knees in pain, clutching his red right hand.

Missed *again*, the voice says. I was aiming for your left hand, Q.

But, J. says in agony, I gave you the correct answer.

Yes, the voice says. But I didn't want to hear the correct answer. I was hoping you'd say seventeen.

But why, J. moans, are you doing this to me? I'm nobody.

To the contrary, Q, the voice says. You are everybody. Now for my next question—

And so on and so forth, Debra would interrupt, that dream means nothing, she would say, but how could it mean nothing J. would banter back, it is just dripping with meaning. So then what is the meaning, Doctor Freud? Debra would ask. How should I know, you're the psychologist with those impressive diplomas, J. would answer. No, Debra would banter back, the only thing it means is that there is something deeply wrong with you but we hardly need to hear your crazy dreams to know that, and so on and so forth.

It's strange what you think about when you are running for your life, J. thought, running, again, not with any plan because what was the point of any plan. Or at least *his* plans because he, pretty clearly, was not running the show around here. He ran out around the building, away from the woods, past the student lodge, there were lights on now but nothing for him there but homicidal maniacal students, on into the Hex, now illuminated, toward the center, those enormous shrubs there, the hedges, the

Maze, he could go hide there, in there, from what, until when, just hide. He ran onto the lawn, toward the hedges, he ran past a girl lying on a wet mattress on the ground sobbing, he wanted to stop, he almost stopped, but couldn't stop, instead he ran alongside the hedges until he found an opening. He plunged in, through it, as if pursued, really pursued, by lunatics, by carnivorous pigs, by *secret histories*. This was no accident, this was not random, he thought, because *someone* had a plan, *someone* was running the show, someone or some many, and it was about him, against him. There was a Department of Conspiracy Values here, no it was Conspiracy Studies, maybe they were involved, they were definitely involved, who else would it be. Find them, expose them, he thought, which Pacman were they in, of course they would just deny it, of course they would, but that would only confirm their complicity. J. ran, he ran, there were some twisting paths through these oversized shrubs but he could not pay attention to details, although *someone* was paying attention to details. He turned, he turned again, there were choices, who the hell planned this, executed this, just choose, don't think, no time for thinking. A right, a left, a three-fold fork, he dove down the middle. Another right and then left, and then he came to a dead end before this enormous—*device*—and stopped.

There was silence.

The full moon was beaming down now well along toward the meridian, the overall scene basking in its silver glow. But the device itself was basking in soft blue spotlights beaming at it from the surrounding stones.

Lost in *dat*, he remembered the student saying.

In the heart of dat.

This *was* dat.

In the blue sheen he could see the device was made of some silvery metal, it was round, it was perched horizontally on a silvery metal stand. Its face was decorated with astronomical or astrological symbols, around its periphery were a dozen images, a lion, a walled city, a set of scales, around those were some

159

compass symbols, there was of course a pair of caterpillars crawling on it, and there was a large triangular protuberance in the center that cast a pattern of bluish shadows over its face, indicating, if this were a clock, and accurately so (although accurate *only* on the night of the full moon, the brochure explained), that it was 11:19 PM.

The Moondial.

More fully, the Philippe Lheureux Memorial Moondial, named after the late early Elder of the college whose bequest had enabled the renovation of the device some fifty-one years earlier.

J. stepped up to it, began reading, in the blue moonlight, the sayings that were carved among the symbols.

Tedious and Brief.

Each Wounds, the Last Kills.

Long Time To Be Gone, Short Time To Be There.

Clusterfuck Of Sorrow.

4500 Hours.

J. stared and stared, wondering what the fuck is happening, wondering how he had come to be at this spot at this time, at the Moondial, in the middle of the Maze, in the middle of the night, near the peak of the full moon, remembering, Robert had told him, that on such nights the students do some ritual at the Moondial, at midnight, which meant the students were on their way here and when they got here they would find him, the Hate they were feverishly attempting to stamp out, the source of all Hate in their minds, all of this seemed to be about getting him to be at this place at this time and all ways seemed to lead here and this was the very last place that he wanted to be but he literally had no idea how to get himself out—

Dammit, he was crying again.

The tears were coming and he was thinking about poor Debra, that sister who wouldn't speak to her after all these years, not even to explain why she wouldn't speak to her, the loss of her mother, still haunting her after all these years, her despicable father who hounded her and now him from even beyond the grave, after all these years, all of them and all of it still crazy after all these years—how remarkable it was that after all Debra had had to endure she had emerged somehow perfect, she was really perfect, she was an endless fount of gorgeous love, this source of truth through and through, and she could be just so devastatingly beautiful when she was vulnerable, it's me Debra Gale all the way down he had said and I would do anything, anything, to make *you* a more permanent feature of my life and give you the family that you deserve that you should have had—

There was a loud rustling and something came thrusting up from the ground before him, in that narrow space between him and the Moondial, grasping his legs and pulling him down.

30

THE WOODS WERE ALIVE this evening. That incredible blitz-storm had dampened their bodies but not their spirits, or at least it was nothing that endless amounts of pomo (and the poco that some well-placed student shadows nicked from the CCP) couldn't fix. This was the best of Nevergreen, the annual Phestival of Phantasmagoria, the reason most of them came here (at least those who had other options), the reason most of them stayed, and that it had all that hate propelling it tonight, that hatred of hate rather, well that was just icing on the cake, the fuel to the fire. That community gathering earlier was rad, mad, dope, legit, awesome, best one ever, really, everyone in solidarity streaming out with their hate-masks to go hate some hate. Over the next two or three hours they were angry, they sought hate, they drank pomo or poco, they got distracted, they discarded their hate-masks and left them wherever, they drank pomo or poco, they took off their costumes and fooled around a little, they got dressed again, they drank pomo or poco. Everyone was psyched for more fooling around after the FOMO party, but first they were psyched for the FOMO party, but first they were psyched for the Midnight Moonshine ritual before the FOMO party, but first still they were psyched to drink this rad mad dope legit awesome poco, which was making them absolutely crazy in all the best senses of the word, and also a little horny. The rain had ended, the full moon was out and rising, the students were streaming all over campus drinking and making out and making up and preparing to reassemble at midnight at the Moondial, and life was just totally phantastic.

Well, not for everyone.

"Go after him!" friend Aaliyah had yelled at Robert when J. disappeared out the third-floor window.

"What, out the window?" Robert said, aghast.

"For virtue's sake, yes!" Luiz shouted.

"Why me? Why not you?" Robert looked at Luiz, who as a strapping young fellow with a flowing mane was certainly more fit than he.

"You are his friend," Aal urged.

"Hardly. I just met him. And frankly now that I have learned more about last night's talk—"

"Just go, Robert," Luiz interrupted. "Before we have—a situation here."

"Hmph. Fine. But I'm taking the elevator."

But by the time Robert had exited the building and made his way to the ferry dock—for he knew J. would try to catch the last boat out—it was too late. The ferry was gone, all that remained was that kid the Colonel of Truth and his goons squabbling about something and threatening each other with air rifles, and no trace of J. to be found.

"He went that way, Professor Merritt," the Colonel answered Robert's query, pointing through the bushes, then returning to his headlock on one of his lackeys.

"That way" was under and through some bushes, so Robert declined to follow suit. Instead he went back along the nearest path, following the stones toward the sanctuary, figuring he would discharge his obligation to the administration by having a general look around the island. The woods were already dark, and it surely didn't help that the clouds were starting to cover the moon. He was reminded of the many tales told of these woods during the years of the asylum: the inmates who believed they were animals, believed they were werewolves, would escape on full moon nights and disappear and never be found. The later rumors about other people vanishing. Could any inmates possibly have managed to get off the island? Robert wondered, feeling the chill of the night. That seemed unlikely, given the currents, but then why weren't the bodies ever found? True, the piglets roaming these woods were thought to be sometimes carnivorous, but that meant small forest animals, mice, chipmunks, the like. They surely couldn't consume an entire human body?

Much less kill it in the first place?

It *was* really chilly, Robert realized, shivering as he tramped through the black woods. He remembered that he was supposed to head back home a while ago, having promised to take his two little ones out around the faculty housing complex behind the gym in Hexant 5. God, that complex was a dump, he thought; its only saving grace was that it was near the barbecue stand. Built nearly a century ago, named for Nevergreen's first President, Professor Christian Rosenkreuz—who in addition to founding the nation's first Department of Conspiracy Studies had had the complex built to house that first wave of German emigré professors who populated the department—it had been due for its first complete renovation just when the budget cuts came five years back. Robert checked his watch, lighting the dial with the button on the side. He was the last man in the mathematics department who still used a watch rather than a phone. Damn it, he muttered, noting that to fulfill his annoying obligation he should probably spend another thirty minutes looking for this fellow before heading home to fulfill his other annoying obligation.

The guy would not likely have gone back into the sanctuary. Maybe down by the beach down there? That was really the only place to go down this way. Robert headed that way, not at all enthused, given what he had heard about the icky things that went on down there. There were students out and about as he approached, doing student things in groups of a few or more. The night felt, what was it, *uneasy.* A storm was coming in, probably. Maybe he should head back to the Hex. It would be really unpleasant to get caught in one of their notorious fall thunderstorms. The administration really couldn't expect him to traipse around through a blitz-storm in search of their fellow.

On the plus side, actually, he thought, hesitating as he walked down toward the beach, a good storm might relieve him of *both* annoying obligations. He was in no rush to get back home, he thought, maybe his wife would take the kids out. It was her turn anyway. After all what did she do around there besides cook and clean and shop for groceries and clothes and maintain the house, organize the finances, arrange the kids' schooling and sports and extracurriculars, and then make love to him like a wild woman half the night long? To think he had wasted those years of his life with that cold witch Orlanda. But then again, it was Orlanda who had introduced him to the young art history department secretary who was now keeping him up half the night. So maybe it was all right, after all.

He thought he heard some screams down by the beach.

Yeah, *that* made a whole lot of sense.

Still, he had been charged with the task of finding this fellow on this island, this fellow who had probably gone down to the beach, and now there were screams down there. It was clearly his obligation to go down to the bottom and get to the bottom of those screams.

"Fuck it," he thought instead, and headed in the opposite direction, up the path and toward the wild woman who was his wife and for whom he found himself very much in the mood.

31

"Aaahh!" J. screamed as the figure came thrusting up from the ground. He jumped back, adopting his best fake kung fu pose acquired from years of fake kung fu-ing with his monsters, determined to put up a stand.

"You damned hobbadehoy!" the little man exclaimed. "You are making a scene!"

J. put down his hands. The strange little librarian who had just popped up from the ground had startled him, but did not seem to pose any fake-kung-fu-worthy threat.

"What scene? There's no one here," J. realized that if he didn't understand the slur the librarian had just flung at him, at least the dramatic entrance had instantly turned off his embarrassing tears.

"No one here? That is rich! They are everywhere," Freinz said incredulously. "Take my hand. I must take you to a safe place." Freinz gazed at him with bulging eyes and a mysterious expression, his arm sticking out of that vest toward J., his hand extended, fingers—crooked, but also, J. noticed, swollen, peeling—beckoning him.

J. hesitated. Trust no one, the man had said earlier. There was too much happening and he surely did not trust anyone, least of all this bizarre little man. Plus it gave him the willies to take that grotesque hand. But then again, he didn't have much choice. The students were on their way and his chances of getting out of this maze alone, much less this mess, were minimal.

"Close the cover, man!" Freinz pulled J. into the tunnel from which he had emerged, then waited for J. to pull the earthen cover back over the opening. "You shall need to crawl, I am afraid. But be quiet. They are listening."

"What is this place?" J. whispered as they began to crawl, their way dully lit by intermittent guidestone-like lights. As he spoke he felt the tears coming back, his voice cracking.

"Less bawl, Doctor," Freinz whispered, slithering ahead of him, "more crawl. All will be revealed in due course. Here it is particularly narrow, I am afraid. We shall have to pull ourselves on our stomachs. Suck it in, Nancy-boy."

Nancy-boy did as he was told. Long minutes went by as they crawled in silence through what was in fact one of the secret tunnels, this one a crawl space between the Crypt below and the Maze above, slowed by the muddy stretches where there were leaks. J.'s mind was racing if his body was not, trying to make sense of the nonsense coming from every direction, willing himself to trust the very man who had warned him to trust no one, but then if he trusted the man he was violating the advice and if he accepted the advice then he couldn't trust the man or the advice ... To distract himself from his circular thoughts he looked up periodically to see the librarian's bony behind in front of him, which set him back into his maze of thoughts. At last they came to a small door with a pushbutton security device. The librarian glanced around, then, with his swollen peeling fingers, punched some eleven buttons. He glanced one more time around, then punched the last button, then pulled J. along by the hand as he pushed open the door.

"Watch your step—" Freinz said as they stumbled into his office.

J. had already fallen the several feet to the floor, adding some bruises to his wounds. He stood up, brushed himself off, then looked back as Freinz slid the Georges de la Tour painting back over the space through which they had just fallen.

"Well that was a pretty neat trick, Mr. Freinz," J. nodded with respect to the man.

"Not as neat as the encore, Doctor," Freinz lifted the top

surface of his desk. With the lifting of the surface everything on it lifted with it, including the papers and books and half-eaten sandwiches and two half-glasses of milk, all of which turned out to be wax simulacra firmly glued down. Inside the desk there was a narrow opening down into which a short ladder led.

"And what's down there?" J. was genuinely curious, momentarily forgetting that he should probably not trust secret passages to unknown destinations.

"Patience, Doctor, all will be revealed," Freinz reached for his leech jar, annoyed with himself that he had diminished the dramatic effect of his reveals by forgetting to do this earlier. "I need a moment please."

"What," J. was confused, "are you going to undertake some hirudotherapy here? Now?" Why not toss back a little arsenic from one of those apothecary bottles on the shelf, while you're at it, J. thought. Maybe have a little—what had he called it—a horn of absinthe, as well? Of course absinthe had a special place in J.'s heart, and his history books, given its connection to Neuchâtel and those splendid chocolates he and Debra shared—

"Shut your bone box a minute, will you, Doctor," the old man snapped, removing a leech from the jar.

"Sorry. Are you actually going to put that thing on yourself?"

"God no, that would be disgusting." Freinz instead brought the leech to his mouth and began sucking on it. "I suck *their* blood," he mumbled over the swollen worm. "It helps with the St. Anthony's Fire. All right, I am good to go. Follow me, Doctor. You shall have to squeeze a little."

At his mercy, J. dutifully followed the little man down the ladder, pulling the desktop back over them as he descended. At the bottom they entered a larger room with a bank of computers and video monitors.

"Welcome to my laboratory," Freinz said majestically as he dwarfed himself into a swivel chair in front of the monitors. "Regard the wires, there, eh, lest you disconnect the generators."

"Your 'laboratory'?" J. stepped over the wires.

"You have a better word, Doctor?"

J. lifted his hands in surrender. "'Laboratory' it is."

"You, my friend," Freinz returned his gaze to the monitors, "are in great danger. Look closely."

Looking over Freinz's shoulder J. saw that some of the monitors' contents were quiet, pastoral, pretty areas of campus, some woods, perhaps the sanctuary, visible even in the dark as the cameras were equipped with night vision lenses. A couple were trained on bedrooms, empty beds all, at least at the moment. J. thought it better not to ask.

But others told a different story.

"What—am I looking at?" J. asked.

"My security cameras," Freinz said proudly.

"*Your* security cameras?"

"Well, the campus security cameras. But these are my hacks."

"You've hacked the campus security system?"

"You sound so surprised, Doctor. What, did you think I lacked the dash-fire to hack the system?"

"No, no," J. lifted his hands again. "Clearly a man of many talents, Mr. Librarian."

"Not that they recognize them here," Freinz muttered, pressing some buttons. "Ah, look, here we are. Ground Naught. Nil, Nul, Cipher."

Freinz pointed a crooked finger at the monitor displaying the blue-bathed Moondial. J. hadn't noticed a camera there, it must have been hidden in the device. That or he'd been too busy weeping over the imminent end of his life. Students were pouring into the central space of the Maze, some still wearing the mask of J.'s face but most having long discarded it, some wearing other masks, some animal face masks, those seemed popular, quite a few pig faces, they were collecting around the Moondial, brightly lit by the blue spotlights and reigning full moon, doing some sort of dance, preparing for some ritual—

"That ninnyhammer!" Freinz exclaimed. "He is obscuring the view!"

A student wearing an impressive Native American headdress had parked said headdress in front of the camera.

"What are they doing?" J. asked uneasily, not liking anything he was seeing.

"You do not want to know, Doctor," Freinz said, clearly relishing the fact that he was about to inform him. "This is the most sacred ritual here, naturally, and given the importance of the near centenary, and the cerulean, well all the more so. I shall say just one word: 'sacrifice.' Do not ask for more. Just be glad they have not found you. Yet."

Strictly speaking that was a lot of words, J. thought, but the librarian had moved on.

"Ah, yes, you, sir, have caused quite the commotion this evening, on our enchanted little island, eh, Doctor?" Freinz could barely suppress the jo-fire in his voice. "I cannot recall the last time the rabble was so roused. See here? How excited they are, setting up for their fizzer after the Howl!" The monitor he was indicating showed students in costumes and masks, reminiscent of Mardi Gras, scurrying around and pumping massive amounts of soapy foam into the Intersections Lounge. "Ah, here we have a sweet and serene scene, eh?" he said, pointing at a monitor showing two, well, *zombies*, entangled in seaweed on the beach, sleeping peacefully. "And here, eh, no time for the jibber-jabber, just right to the gobble-do-gee, ma'am," he said, pointing at two women dressed up as female genitalia doing things that J. might have liked to examine more closely had circumstances been rather entirely, completely different. "Ah, well, now, look here who has gotten a little skeery," Freinz muttered, pointing to another monitor. "Somebody is jumping ship."

"Who is that?" Several people were loading onto a boat but the night vision was fuzzy.

"The private dock, Doctor, far side of the cliffs. There goes Bob, with some deputies. Of course. I should have anticipated."

"Bob?" J. tried to make out the President he had not yet seen. That was odd, it was hard to be sure but didn't that rather look like Brenda, was that the sweater—

"Cowards, the whole lot," Freinz shook his head, clearly distracted by something. "But it is all part of the plan. I should have anticipated."

"Anticipated what? What is happening?"

"You cannot trust a single scoundrel in this place," Freinz continued shaking his disheveled white hair, pressing buttons. "Ah, but now look, Doctor, *these* delightful specimens are underway with their roast. Look here. And here. A man can live for this, Doctor. The adrenaline does wonders for the scrofula."

Freinz pointed at two different monitors. J. never got to look at the second because his gaze was fixed on the first. It was that group of students in the sanctuary, stripped down, streaks of face-stripe and body paint. They were doing some violent dance around a fire pit in which—Freinz helpfully zoomed in on the image—an entire, if headless, piglet was roasting on a spit. "Let us have some volume, shall we?" Freinz slid a dial next to the monitor.

"Drink its blood!" the students chanted as they danced. "Drink its blood!"

"Charming, eh, Doctor? Just be glad they have not found you either. Yet. Have a gander at this, my friend, to see what you are dealing with. A short while ago." The old man was practically beside himself as he swiveled to an adjacent monitor then rewound the recording. "Ah, here we are! Let us zoom. This fellow is quite the masterpiece and you should not want to miss the bulging even of a single muscle. And, play!" He dialed the volume up and pressed the button.

"Men," Zeke was hissing to his fellow carnivores in a clearing in some woods. "We have hunted the piglet. We have removed its head. And we have smeared ourselves with its blood, which we shall drink—or how do you say it—chugalug at midnight."

"Drink its blood!" they chanted. "Drink its blood!"

Zeke put up his bloody hand to silence them. "What remains, I ask myself? What yet must I do?"

"You?" someone asked. "Or all of us?"

"All of us! But especially me. Anyone? Anyone?"

There was a long silence.

"The ultimate end?" Zeke suggested. "The final frontier? The Holy Grail for every carnivore? Anyone?"

More silence.

"Very well, then. I, the Man of Meat," Zeke's voice began to tremble, "I speak of—"

"The Meat of Man," a powerful voice boomed out.

"Right you are, Benjo," Zeke felt the blood coursing through his veins as much by what was said as by who had said it. He stared his carnivorous stare at his soon to be consecrated protégé. "Tonight, indeed, I seek: the Meat of Man."

J. was too busy thinking about the librarian's use of the word "yet" to have absorbed the remark about the portending cannibalism. His stomach was turning as much from the image of the headless piglet as from the immediately suggested image of his own headless body roasting on that spit.

"Are they—talking about me?" J.'s voice trembled too, now absorbing the threat.

"We can only hope," Freinz's eyes bulged.

"I'm sorry?"

"Ah! Did I say that aloud? Pay no—"

"What," J. interrupted, "exactly did I do? I don't understand."

"Listen here, Doctor," Freinz said almost wistfully, and not unkindly, as he furrowed his brow. "It is not anything you did. It is who you are. It is what you are."

"But what am I?"

"You," Freinz pointed a crooked finger at him, "are Hate."

"How—what does that mean? I'm a middle-aged doctor suffering from maybe a midlife crisis. I have a wife who has grown tired of me and three monstrous children. I like classic rock. I occasionally bowl."

"There you have it," Freinz said.

"Have what?"

"The Hate."

"How is that 'hate'?"

"'The Hate,' capital T, capital H."

"How am I 'The Hate'?!" J. spluttered.

"The fact that you do not know is itself The Hate. The fact that you must ask, is The Hate," Freinz said firmly now. "Doctor, they know you. And you have much to learn. Look here. We return to the Moondial."

One of the monitors now featured, front and center, Dr. Taslitz M. Fester, sitting in his wheelchair, surrounded by swarms of maddened students.

"Shall we raise the volume again, Doctor, as the midnight hour has at last arrived, and the good Doctor may, at long last, be ready to break his silence?"

Freinz also zoomed in so that the face of Dr. Taslitz M. Fester filled the screen, the round face, the almond eyes, the small dark mole a punctuation mark on his dark skin, the full lips as the old man opened them finally to speak—

32

BUT WHAT CAME OUT of those lips were not words, not words in any language you could understand though perhaps words in some secret language, some language of secrets ... not speech exactly but a long, loud, guttural, gut-busting, soul-scorching, animalistic, across the campus, through the woods, over the waters, across time and space, it was a howl, it was a howl, it was a HOWL ...

A HOWL—

"What the hell—" J. stuttered, grasping, covering his ears at the volume of the thing as all the assembled students, there must have been hundreds crammed into that blue-dipped space, in their outfits, their masks, as they joined in, joined the howl, the HOWL ...

"Oh, that is bad," Freinz said, clearly thinking it was good while turning down the volume as the howl continued. "That is very, very bad, Doctor. I understand now why Bob jumped ship."

"What? What is happening?"

Freinz swiveled his chair back to J., bulged his eyes at him, his brows crumpled. "You, my friend, are happening. *It* is happening. This is very, very goo—" Freinz caught himself, "bad. Very bad."

"What does that mean?"

"The next vessel out of here is at 7:13 AM. Eighteen minutes after dawn. That means we have about—" he pulled his time-piece from the vest-pocket—"eight hours and eight and a half minutes we need to keep you alive."

"It's just after midnight. Don't you mean seven hours?"

"Clock change tonight," Freinz answered smugly.

"Ah. More importantly. What the fuck does that mean, 'keep me alive'?"

"There is no time to explain, Doctor. It is good you came to me. Now come along. I know just the place to stash you."

As if he had a choice? J thought, following the man, who suddenly had yip-fire in his step, back up the ladder, back into his office. The man grabbed a thin-beam flashlight then moved out into the darkened corridor where they made their way to some back stairs in the Depository, up the stairs that climbed and climbed until they came out into a pitch-dark corridor several floors above the librarian's office. The librarian reached around him to press a small button no one would notice if they didn't know where to look for it.

"I installed these myself," Freinz said as some dim lights came on, in the tone of a man in the habit of not getting credit for his many talents. The corridor they were in was lined by tall shelves filled with books in every direction. "Now follow me. In the 'B' section I have stored some cushions, a flashlight, some tins. You will be safe up here. Nobody comes here anymore."

A few minutes later Freinz had parked him between some shelves, with some cushions to rest on and canned victuals to survive on.

"I—well, thank you," J. said.

Freinz nodded. "I shall retrieve you at half past six to escort you to the vessel. You will be safe up here." He paused, then bulged his eyes meaningfully at J. "You will remain here, will you not? No more gallivanting about?"

"You know," J. ventured, "you can get treatment for that."

"For what?"

"The proptosis. The—bulging—"

Freinz glared at him. "I am good, thank you, Doctor. Now. No more gallivanting about, shall we say?"

"Of course," J. yielded, feeling alarmed by the librarian's manner. "You saw the monitors. Where the hell else could I go?"

"Very well, then, Doctor. And now I shoo. Adieu!"

The librarian did something resembling a curtsy then disappeared down the corridor, leaving J. to spend what remained of the ghastly night in the library stacks. There was something odd about that exchange, J. thought, in the first twenty-five minutes he spent trying to fall asleep, perturbed first at the, well, the *finality* of the farewell, the abrupt "Adieu!," then second at the unexpected failure of his normally legendary ability to fall asleep anywhere; and then, third, after the long trail of ruminations finally led him to recall that when he had been at the Museum of Curiosities, staring at that poster, there had been a small acknowledgment at the bottom that the exhibit was designed and installed by none other than one Johann S. Freinz, Head Librarian.

Trust no one, the old man said.

Most definitely including him.

33

FREINZ SLINKED DOWN THE hallway after setting J. up for the night, following the beam of his flashlight through the narrow stacks. Setting J. up for the night indeed, he thought, feeling satisfied, very satisfied, that his plan was working perfectly. The damned fool trusted him like a puppy dog, was settling in for the night, there was no rush, no rush at all. He made his way back to his laboratory, thought he may as well enjoy a last look at the monitors as he determined the precise details of the next step. A study of the state of the campus, yes the state of the campus, at—he checked his timepiece—12:47 AM, only forty-three minutes to the meridian. He settled into the chair, began pressing buttons. That silly fool was up in the lair, reading his phone, not going anywhere. At this hour the major campus event would be the FOMO party, just underway with the Howl howled. Most of the students had left the Moondial, were pouring into the lounge. Yes, that party was quite the soirée, who knew exactly what those barmy students were up to, with all that fimble-famble foam obscuring the lenses. Tonight, tonight, it was all coming together, after his many disappointments over his years here. Time was, way back, that libraries were not merely relevant but essential. He had status here, he was a *Big Dog*. "The Librarian" had such a pleasant ring to it, particularly when there were so many librarians at that time but only one "The Librarian." But now that they were all gone and he truly was "the" librarian those other Big Dogs, the Big Dogs who ran this place, had repeatedly declined his requests to make "The Librarian" his official title. He was pissing against the wind, he knew. Libraries were more museums now than anything else, his rank in the great scheme of things only sinking. His eyes roamed to the monitors covering the outstanding exhibit he had conceived, designed, executed for the college. Well all right, Dr. Fester had wheeled by and dropped off that book of his, the one inspired by the earlier scholar who first tracked the history of that caterpillar book, which in turn inspired Fester to uncover its secret history. But it was him, Freinz, who got the idea of the exhibit based on the book, and brought it into being.

And what was the response?

Gullyfluff, Freinz thought bitterly.

The administrators didn't even bother coming to the opening. Never mind the President, the Vice President, the Provost, the academic deans, the values deans; not even the vice deans, the deputy deans, the vice-deputy deans, out of how many dozens of administrators, these people who sucked the budget dry leaving nothing for anyone else, certainly nothing for the librarian who not only had stopped acquiring physical books several years back but had stopped acquiring even the catalogs from which to order those books. Not a single one had shown up, too busy budget-sucking to show a splinter of respect, or even interest, in anyone else. Freinz realized he had forgotten his apophlegmatism again, pulled out his sneezer, blew. Had to be more consistent on that, he thought, remembering that a handful of faculty had wandered in to the opening but were more interested in the food than in the exhibit itself. Only one student showed up, that young woman-man (it was not clear) he would sometimes bump into on the first floor who he thought looked at him almost with, well, how could one reliably interpret a face if one could not even reliably interpret the sex? Was the expression bemusement, was it contempt, could it possibly be, he liked to think it was, *respect*? But then she or he would look away and disappear. Never mind the Big Dogs, never mind the Medium Dogs, basically no Dogs showed up because it was just an exhibit put together not by The Librarian but by the librarian and the librarian was no longer relevant, not at all.

Until tonight, Freinz thought, his eyes glimmering in a way they hadn't in—years. What a fine shake of the elbows that was, for him, that the personification of Hate had arrived on his own decaying campus and ended up in his control. He had played the situation beautifully, he thought. Freinz glanced at the monitor, could see J. had turned off the light, was tossing and turning up in the stacks, all innocent, unaware.

Well, now, maybe, at last, they would appreciate him around here.

That little colt, Bacharo, his untamed locks always flowing, he was the one to bet on, he knew it. He was on to the man from the beginning, the scheming, the meteoric rise through the ranks of the administration, always lip-smacking the right sitters, always the right place, right time. Freinz's attention was drawn to a monitor on which several students wearing puffy white outfits were starting to dig a large pit, a fire pit, just behind the library, *his* library. Those cussed fools were going to burn this place down one year, he thought, resolving, once again, to give them a good anointing once he had the authority to do so. And that, precisely, was what Bacharo was going to provide, he thought, swiveling in the chair, tenting his swollen crooked fingers.

Bacharo had already eliminated his immediate superior, Rava, crushing her with that delightful show outside the Teach-In. That whole play with the student shadow, ha! A play it was, a performance, that whole shadow system was Bacharo's doing, he was calling the shots all along. And now the President had flown the coop, gone, too, things were too hot to handle, the things Bacharo himself had heated up, and that left only the Vice President, whom Bacharo already had wound around his finger, which meant now, of course, there really was only one Big Dog here, at least below the Elders, Bacharo was in charge, the coop was flown and the coup was complete—and now his own plan was ready for its moment, its realization …

Bacharo hated hate. And now everyone in this god-forsaken

loony bin hated hate with him. And he, The Librarian, had Hate in his control, and when the time was right, would yield up that Hate to this frothing crowd for its proper exflunctication. Ah, the expressions on those hysterical faces, Freinz imagined, when he would lead the students to this cozy den where that evil man was tossing and turning. He would have to ensure a good clear camera angle, to record it for posterity. And ditto, again, when he made it clear, to Big Dog Bacharo, that it was he, The Librarian, who had made it all happen.

When the time was right, he thought, consulting his timepiece again: 1:23 AM. Almost the meridian. There was no rush, almost seven whole hours, he had the whole night ahead. He would relish this, enjoy this, continue to monitor the scene for now, the students were spreading out again over the campus, there was much to monitor. In a little while, there was no rush, he would climb back up and have a horn of absinthe from the bottle on his shelf, to help with that small stone in his cranium that lately he had begun to feel growing, pressing, swelling. The headaches, the dizziness, the thoughts, they were getting increasingly difficult to deal with, he thought. And then, when the time was right, he would set off in search of just the right group of overexcited students to let them know where they could find the Hate they were seeking and were so eager to exfluncticate.

Meanwhile the librarian turned his attention back to the monitors on the lounge, tried to make out precisely what was happening. Just what in the devil's wages were they up to, underneath all that fimble-famble foam?

34

HE WAS SO UNBELIEVABLY tired, tired to the bone, in the bones, but sleep was unlikely here, now, even for him. So alone in the silence, in the darkness, under the stream of the lamp clipped to the bookshelf. J. tossed against the cushions the librarian had provided. Something was bothering him about the way the man left him, that sharp "Adieu!" like the stab of a knife. J. pulled out his phone, thought about calling Debra, it was too late, or too early with the time difference, she would think he was crazy, maybe he was. He passed some minutes at the Resistance website reading the stories that the Cerise-Verisce alliance had been posting all day about the hate he had brought to this campus, then reading through the hundreds of appended comments from around the world. Seven and a half hours to the boat that would rescue him, he thought as he skimmed through the hostility. Journey to the end of the night, he thought. Death on the installment plan. Good slogans for the Moondial. Perhaps there was a suggestion box somewhere. If not then he would suggest they have one. He could not tell if that was clever or just stupid. Such a fine line, Debra would say. It was so late, he was so tired. See here, he thought, how everything led up to this day. It was just like any other day that had ever been, and yet—all of it, not just today, not just meeting Brenda on the plane, but starting back then, meeting Debra, her father, that book, that exhibit, her dying mother, the Neuchâtels and the absinthe, absinthe makes the heart grow fonder, such a fine line, he just loved the way she got to the essence of everything, all of it, was it all aimed to produce—*this*? It was not possible, it just was not possible, and yet everything, everything that had been seemed connected to everything that now was, and would be, or should be, oh would and should do make you ill …

It was dusty in here, he thought, cobwebby, hard to breathe. The littlest monster would be miserable here, with the thick air, the hard floor, smelly cushions. But then again the littlest monster would be miserable anywhere—

There. He blinked. He had been skimming one of the Resistance petitions against him circulating the world, demanding he suffer depredations, punishments, Jesus there were hundreds of signatures on that thing, scrolling down, scrolling down, and there it was.

Robert Merritt.

What the fuck.

Why did this hurt so much … Who was this guy, he was no different from anyone else, clearly, no one to be trusted here—that's what the librarian had said, the librarian who had rescued him from the Moondial, who, now that he thought about it, was eager for J. to come to him, when it happens, he had said, you must return here, it is good you came to me, you will remain here. Those comments struck him as strange at the time, but who had time to process strange comments when the world was on fire around you? Stay here, do not gallivant, he had said, the strange little man, the strange little man—it suddenly hit J. that when he was at the Museum of Curiosities, staring at that poster, there was a small note at the bottom that the exhibit had been designed and installed by none other than one Johann S. Freinz, Head Librarian.

There would be no rest here, J. knew.

Instantly he snapped off the light. As if that would keep him safe, the man, that man, he could see in the dark, if he put together that exhibit then he was in on it, all of it, this plot, it all led up to this day, this moment.

Where could he go? He had nowhere to go.

He closed his eyes. Waited a few minutes. Pretend to be asleep, toss and turn, that was a plan. It may not have been a good plan, but it was a plan. The guidestone cameras were equipped for night vision but perhaps the indoor cameras were not. If they were, then maybe after a few minutes of seeing him asleep the librarian's attention would go elsewhere. It was hard to know how much time elapsed since he did not want to turn on his phone. And the battery was very low. After an eternity of darkness and silence, breathing in the cobwebby air, he realized that tossing and turning were not a plan at all.

He had nowhere to go yet could not stay here.

Another Moondial slogan he thought.

J. lifted himself from the recline, quietly, began crawling, toward the end of the aisle. Best to stay low, as quiet as possible. There were microphones too, remember. He made it to the end of the aisle, the world did not end, not yet. He continued crawling down the corridor along the outside edges of the bookshelves. It struck him that there was no point in crawling, if there were night-vision cameras here then he would be seen whether standing or crawling. He stood, listened, crept forward. No sirens, no lights, no howling. The old man was maybe not paying attention, perhaps he was asleep. Even Elders had to sleep, no?

J. continued down the corridor until he came to a small circular staircase he hadn't noticed earlier. He could not stay here and there was no other place on campus to go, so concealing himself higher up in the stacks seemed the best plan. There was a creak as he took the first step on the stairs. To him the creak was a conch or ram's horn sound that beckoned the entire world to gather about *him*. He stood frozen on the bottom step for at least one lifetime, he thought. A deer stuck in the headlights, and he was the deer though there were no lights, it was all in the darkness. After a while the silence and the darkness, the circle, remained unbroken.

He carried on.

The wheels of virtue were turning, Aal said, Bob said. When

the wheels are turning you can't slow down, he thought. But you also can't let go and you can't hold on. You can't go back and you can't stand still. So on, and up, he went, for no reason other than that he couldn't do nothing and moving on, and up, were at least something. The circular staircase took him up two more flights, then a third. This may have been the top floor of the stacks. He imagined the roof, a helipad, a helicopter swooping in for a dramatic rescue. Then he imagined perhaps watching fewer stupid movies. Debra was always complaining about his picks—

As he came off the stairs it occurred to him to resume crawling again in the corridor before him, but then he remembered his earlier point about the night-vision cameras. But then again, could night-vision cameras operate in the *complete* darkness? He hadn't taken the flashlight the librarian left for him below. Of course the man *would* leave a flashlight, the better to follow J. should he attempt to escape. How quickly J. kept falling back into, what, *credulity*, that was the word Debra used, he was always doing that, so easy to be taken advantage of, but really isn't that better overall than to build a wall around yourself, to push away, he would say, and so they would banter. Stay focused, J. reminded himself, do not use the librarian's flashlight, and anyway probably night-vision cameras could operate in the complete darkness. But then again—

It was not completely dark.

Several aisles ahead there was a light.

Like a moth drawn toward the light—were caterpillars also drawn to light?—J. found himself drawn. No, like an insect drawn toward the zapper that would end it, he thought, more apt. There were no bug-zappers for the damn caterpillars, they had killed them with the fungus and then managed the fungus with the pigs, the pigs that were hunted tonight, their heads cut off, by the pig-zappers. J. shook his own head to shake away the thoughts as he crept down the corridor, in stealth mode, drawn, pulled, reaching for the imaginary pistol he did not have. He crept down the corridor, past darkened aisle after aisle, coming to the aisle of bookshelves right before the aisle that was illumi-nated, illuminatus, illuminati, he stopped, he stopped thinking, stopped breathing, peered between the books in the shelves—

There was a person in there.

35

"IT'S ALL RIGHT," THE gentle, vaguely familiar voice said. "You are safe here. I have diverted the camera."

J. stepped around the corner into the small circle of light, saw the young woman who had set herself up in the aisle there.

"It's all right," she said again, seeing him. "You are safe here."

"I know you," J. breathed a little.

"You do."

"I know you. But. Different."

"It's all right. Take your time."

J. inhaled, exhaled. "The driver. You brought me here. But you look—different."

She nodded. "In the raw," she said with a soft lisp, putting her hands out palm up. "Unplugged. As God made me. As I am."

"I can't say I understand."

"It's all right. Have a seat," she gestured to a stool next to the one she was seated on, adjacent to a pile of books many of which had post-it notes sticking out from various pages. As J. gratefully accepted her offer she pointed to her jaw. "What is different?"

"No—hint of beard?"

"Points for observation skills. So what follows?"

"You are a woman?"

"Points for inference skills! Under normal conditions that would be an excellent conclusion. But here at Nevergreen?"

"Nothing is assumed. Anything follows."

She nodded. "When I began here, as a cis-girl, almost nobody spoke to me. I was basically just a loser. After a while I realized I could raise my social capital by pretending to be a boy. That was pretty awesome until, well, it seemed like everyone was pretending to be the opposite sex. So that's when I started pretending to be a boy who was pretending to be a girl."

"And?"

"Most popular kid on campus."

"And now?" J. gestured to her beardless jaw.

She smiled. "It's really tiring to be the most popular kid on campus. And the makeup is a lot of work. Not to mention that grunting thing boys always do. I come up here just to be myself."

"But you work for the college," J. reminded himself to be skeptical. "You drive."

"A girl has to eat."

"You have—three stools here," J. noted, suspiciously.

"There are others."

"You are not alone."

"Not entirely. No."

"You said you—diverted the camera?" J.'s gaze wandered as he said this.

"Here," she pointed to a shelf with a tiny lens just visible. "Yes. I'm handy. This feed now shows one of the classics aisles instead. *Very* quiet."

J. exhaled deeply, against his better judgment, but how good that deep breath felt. "My name is J.," he said softly.

"I know."

"And yours?"

"Elijah. Pleasure to actually meet you. In the raw." She extended her hand.

"Elijah?" J. took her hand, re-reminding himself of his better judgment.

"Confusing, I know. My parents are missionaries. Yes, there are still missionaries. Supersessionist silliness, the whole package. You can't imagine the teasing I got in school."

"But you are a—a girl."

"I know, I know. They picked the name before I was born.

They had high hopes for me. I was their dream. You don't aban-
don a dream just because reality doesn't cooperate, now do you?"

J. gazed at her, illuminated by the little lamp against the
blackness of the surrounding bookshelves, aisles, stacks, world.

"You are Elijah," he pointed at her. "You work with—"

"Professor Thatch. Exactly. No fear. *She* would never sign
any petitions." She gazed back at him. "Hey, you. Why so glum,
chum? You look like you could use some tea?" She gestured
toward a hotpot she had stashed on the shelf behind her between
some books.

"Would I like some tea," J said, would he like some tea, was
that so obvious, tea with a splash of milk he thought, this young
woman wouldn't have milk here but that was how Debra would
take it, because that was how her mother took it, their thing
with tea, the green tea perfume, how he came to love that scent
on Debra, not just because of the scent but because of what it
meant, it was her love for her mother, it was remarkable, that
love, the source of her gorgeous love, himself he was a coffee
man, but would he like some tea now. He settled in, to the night,
for the night, feeling at ease, or almost at ease. Was there some
commotion downstairs at some point, murmurs and shouts, mur-
derous bellows, she said it's all right, you are safe here, and began
describing her work with Professor Thatch. Thatch was a subver-
sive, who would have guessed, her day job focused on the history
of female yadda-yadda, across all times and cultures, except for
the one time and culture that really mattered to her, which she
reserved for her night job, and didn't tell them or anyone about
because no one would understand, no one would accept, they
would raise roadblocks, get in her way, shut her down. J. couldn't
quite follow, there were unfamiliar terms, languages, something
about the Book of Memory, the Book of King Solomon, the
shechinah, something about the desert she said, was there a desert
area on the island maybe, and there was something else, Dinah,
the rape, Susanna, she said, or a book of that name. No, J. did
not follow the details nor the references nor the foreign words

as they streamed over him, but Thatch had been working on this for many years, only her most trusted student assistants were to know, she believed there were enormous metaphysical and maybe metapolitical implications for this or that or the yadda-yadda but there were great enemies out there opposed to the work, opposed to the truth, resisting it, the resistance. You see it all rode, *all* of it, on whether a particular ancient smudge on a particular ancient parchment discovered in some particular ancient cave was merely a smudge or deliberate, because then one letter would or should actually be a different letter, which would or should then change the word, which would or should then change the passage, which would and should then change *absolutely everything about everything* ...

"Change everything...?" J. was sleepy, the tea was making him drowsy. "I don't understand. From what? To what?"

"It's all right," Elijah said, "be patient, I will explain."

"It's so—late," J.'s eyes were drooping, the commotion, died down, he was lost, in the conversation, in space and time, so tired.

"It's all right, it's only two, you have time. You are safe here. More tea, you'll feel better."

She poured, she refilled, had he drunk his cup already, she explained that the secret was not in what was there but in what wasn't there, in the smudge or not-smudge, what should be there, it is about connecting the dots, she said, there are always dots, and there are always connections. She was herself a metachemistry student with interests in classics and calligraphy or was it metaclassics with interests in calligraphy and chemistry, she was studying the smudge's chemical properties, they had smuggled some of the ink out, they had scraped and smuggled, Indiana Thatch, and there were snakes because there always were snakes, they were having it analyzed, what properties it had, what properties it should have had, it was endless, the dots were endless, the connections. Most nights found her here, she said, sometimes with the others when campus was particularly crazy, when *they* were particularly crazy, but usually alone, where she could read and think, or think and drink, some green tea, green tea the healthiest beverage on the planet the antioxidants and the rest, it was the second two AM and there still was time, she said, it was all right, he should relax, he should drink his tea, he was safe here. She told J. how when she first started hiding here at night she would imagine getting locked in the library, almost fantasize about it, sort of. It could happen, after all. Students never came here anymore, there was a skeletal staff, mostly just the librarian, he was eccentric you know and not to be trusted, the cameras, he was probably in cahoots with Bacharo, watch out for him too, but anyway, the skeletal staff, at some point they would just lock the whole place up and throw away the key. She imagined having all that time, all the time in the world, to explore the place, she would head downstairs, down, rumors told of hidden tunnels that connected the library to other places on campus, led down to cellars, dungeons, from the asylum days. Word was there was a room down there with all the devices used to "encourage compliance" (they used to say) from the less compliant inmates, this chamber of horrors was named the Knox Behavioral Modification Room in memory of the first (apparently quite sadistic) warden of the asylum. She imagined getting lost down there, underground somewhere, or maybe even back upstairs, in the stacks, maybe even the classics section, *very* quiet there, with all the time in the world there was time to lose yourself anywhere. She might fall in some deserted corner and her body remain there for months or years until everything changed, everything about everything, when perhaps some fresh adventurous first-year might find her way in here and follow her trail and retrace her steps and find her skeleton lying there, recognizable only by the mahogany-framed eyeglasses perched on the bony nose and the rotted satchel strapped over the crumbling shoulder. Okay, so she didn't actually wear glasses, but if she did they would be mahogany-framed. J. was so sleepy he didn't want any more tea he liked the way she said that, it was something Debra would say, he always did love the way Debra thought and he rather liked the way this young woman thought, too, as she described her nights up here in the stacks, in her safe space where she could read and think and be as God made her, among the books, surrounded by the books, she would run her finger along their spines and read the titles, she said, imagining they could announce their names out loud, like Siri or Alexa or, even better, she imagined, what if instead of the books on the shelves there were the authors themselves? Shelf after shelf, crouched-over men and women barking their wares, competing for her attention, trying to sell their titles, their theses, their arguments?

"God is nature and the implications are staggering," one might shout from the bottom shelf.

"Homer was a woman!" another might shout from the other side. "And what's more—*her name wasn't Homer!*"

"The humour, the humour," a third bellows from above, "it *is* the pus!"

These were familiar, these examples, were they from Dr. Taslitz Fester, some of them, yes Dr. Fester she said, it all starts with Dr. Fester, perhaps ends with Dr. Fester, they love Dr. Fester here, the howl, the howler, his career, his books, apparently a whiz in the kitchen too, specialty beverages, his memoir the source for the pomo recipe even. He was once a very nice rooster to be around but one day it was over, six years ago, he stopped speaking, he stopped writing, his labors unfinished, for reasons unknown, I shall write no more, he wrote, the penultimate words, the final words, for I have seen that the world is straw. That's it, J. asked, that's it, she answered. What does that mean J. asked. How should I know she said, how should anyone know, the labors are unfinished for reasons unknown, now he just gurgles and growls and howls, and they love it here, they eat it up, they digest it, they defecate it. Sorry was that gross she said, with that gentle lisp, he looked at her medium-length hair, her smooth face, she was really, was she really, he was so tired, it's okay he said, hey, he said, hey you. Yes she said. Why are you telling me all this now, he said. Well you're the one here aren't you she said, a nice banter that. No I mean you were sort of cold to me in the car and now this so what is different. What is different she said, only everything. Now I know who you are, then, who were you, you were someone Bob was bringing in, you were probably one of them. No it wasn't Bob he said it was Brenda, I met her on the plane, Brenda who then disappeared on me here. No, silly, she said, Brenda *is* Bob, Brenda O'Brien, they call her BOB here, you really didn't know? Brenda *is* Bob, he said, Brenda *is* Bob, she said, Brenda is Bob is Brenda is Bob is Brenda he thought again, and again, as the night went on, deeper into the dark, rounding the corner perhaps, there couldn't be much time before the dark began to weaken, to yield, to the first wisps of dawn, gray smoky wisps curling upward, thickening, thickening—J. was losing track of everything, of the hordes, they're just kids, that crazy librarian who was going to rat him out, to smoke him out, yes to smoke him out, he was becoming aware that something was burning, something, somewhere. Paper, books, the burning of books, where they start with burning books they end with burning people, who said that, a saying, no, this was today, this year, the year of the, what, they don't burn books anymore, not here, not now, it was acrid, bitter, it was something else, it was—insects, the smell of burning insects, of burning—*caterpillars?* What would he know of that, had he smelled that smell before, was this just his imagination, or could it be, he thought as he snapped alert, his eyes shooting wide open, as he realized, could this be possible—

The library was on fire.

36

In Freinz's laboratory the monitors were continuing to live-stream the state of the campus. The FOMO party was long over, the lounge mostly empty except for some slowly evaporating foam and a handful of students undressed to different degrees and sleeping off the good time. The Moondial was deserted once more except for some trash, some vaping paraphernalia left behind, to remain largely unvisited again until next month's rituals. The carnivores' cookout was done, the meal consumed, the bellies full and digesting, some dying embers contributing a last glow to that of the soon-to-be setting moon. The most exciting action was on the monitor showing the laboratory itself, for there was the infinitely looped representation of itself within itself, including the top of the swivel chair in front of the monitor where the mop of disheveled white hair was rising and sinking with each subsequent snore; had the volume been turned up then the infinite sound loop would also have included that forgot-again-to-take-his-apophlegmatism phlegmatic snore. The only thing really happening on campus was the bonfire behind the Depository, built by the members of the Marshmallow Club, still smarting from the beating at the gathering, for their annual post-Howl Grand Roast. Once again that idiot Hillman, their self-declared Grand Mallow after last year's coup overthrew that idiot Shenton, had screwed up: the by-laws *explicitly* stated the fire was to begin at dawn, but the idiot read the chart wrong *again* and started it twenty-five minutes early. Well perhaps it was good he did, because the wet wood took some time to catch, but catch it did just ten minutes before dawn, and was now producing a thick, heavy, smoky flame. With an arsenal of speared marshmallows ready for roasting, they were drinking their by-laws-mandated warmed-up elixir of honey and pomo as they prepared for the primal screaming ritual that went with the roast. The Depository stacks themselves were of course empty, quiet, abandoned, except for that one monitor showing a close-up of J.'s face, his eyes wide open in fear, his nostrils twitching, and some spittle dangling from the corner of his mouth.

"Sweet Mother Jesus!" J. exclaimed, channeling his father for some reason, the smell of the smoke in his nostrils. Earth, North America, Northwest, Grand Island, Nevergreen, Depository, stacks: it took a moment to remember where he was. Then a moment longer to remember that the library was on fire and unless he wanted to meet Sweet Mother Jesus in person, which he most certainly did not, it was time for him to start moving.

Sweet Mother Jesus forgive me, he thought as he began running, thinking it was probably sinful to not want to meet the alleged savior in person now, or any time soon, really. There was that story told about the famous physicist Neils Bohr, hyper-rational, dismissive of superstition, yet who used to keep some aboriginal good luck amulet on his office door. "But Neils," someone (was it Einstein?) once asked him, "why do you have that on your door? You don't believe in that nonsense." "I don't," Bohr replied, "but I heard it also works for people who don't believe in it." It's funny what you think of as you run for your life, J. thought, running for his life.

It was slow going, it was still dark, but he got out of the aisle, down the corridor, couldn't find the circular staircase. Other way, he thought, the other stairs, finding them, his fear intensifying as the smoke smell intensified in his descent. Could this be, he thought, they were trying to—smoke him out? By setting fire to the whole library? That seemed excessive, even for them. More than what keeping it crazy would absolutely require. He descended in the dark, I'm going down, he thought, shouldn't there be sprinklers in here or something? He got down the staircase, out of the inverted abyss that was the stacks, to the first floor of the Depository. There were some lights here, the smoke was thicker, but he realized he hadn't actually seen the flames as he paused a moment for breath, for a smoky breath, and looked at his phone, its battery almost dead: 6:27 AM. Out the window, there were windows here, there was air out there, it was mostly dark but he could see, just see, the first streaks of dawn.

If he left now—if he moved quickly—if he didn't get lost—if he weren't captured—speared, roasted, eaten—he could make it to the dock for the morning boat out of here.

So move quickly he did, past the closed Coffée Bar, past the desolate Information Desk, past the main doors to the Intersections Lounge out of which a young woman with bleary severe eyes was emerging, wearing nothing but some foam barely covering her private parts, not at all sure what she had been doing the past six hours but entirely sure it was worth it. There was plenty of smoke but it wasn't obvious where the actual fire was. He ran toward the main entrance of the Depository but saw students there, loitering, lingering, vaping. Didn't seem so threatening but then again he couldn't take a chance so he turned around, went back through the corridors Freinz had led him through yesterday, skirted around the librarian's office, toward that rear exit the librarian had shown him, sure enough, another corridor and there was the door all the way in the back with the words "Emergency Exit" painted on it.

Time to pull foot, he thought, and went to push.

It didn't move.

Perhaps the goddamn librarian had pulled his leg instead, he thought. But then he saw there was a combination lock with twelve goddamn alphabetic chambers on it that surely had not been there yesterday, that surely that goddamn librarian had imposed there to trap his prey.

That proptosic, ergotic, scrofulic bastard, he thought, channeling his mother who could curse a blue streak whenever somebody crossed her but who, in fact, had never harmed a soul in her life and was still the kindest, most gentle person he had ever known, although Debra was a close second of course, although why was he thinking of them right now when he was trying to escape a maybe burning building, but Debra, Debra really was the love of his life, his monsters, his kids, maybe were not a disaster, the kids are alright really, well if these were to be his last thoughts—

Twelve-letter combination, he thought, no idea, blanks. In desperation he tried the first thing to mind, punching in the letters T-H-E-L-I-B-R-A-R-I-A-N.

The lock clicked open.

J. would have shaken his head if he had had time to do anything other than what he did do, which was push open the door and pull foot.

He had successfully evaded that student straggling out of the lounge, he had successfully escaped the vapers out front, only now to eject himself—if *defenestrate* was through the window, what would through a door be, door in Latin, *porta*—only now to *deport* himself directly into the middle of a thick smoky horde of students holding little spears, little burning spears spearing small mounds of sticky burning flesh, making the most blood-curdling screams he had heard at least since last night.

What happened to Elijah, he suddenly thought, realizing she hadn't been there when he smelled the smoke and launched his escape.

Was she still up there?

There was no time to think about that, he thought, and took off down the path stretching from the rear of the Depository just as the smoky horde of they're-just-kids turned its flesh-searing attention to him.

37

Wrong way! Wrong way!

Wherever that voice in his head came from there was no time to question it, he turned around, found the outside path, the path that ran around the perimeter of the Hex and most of the island. The brochure in his pocket noted that the path was variably called the Outer Limit, the Outer Circle, or simply the Areola, depending on who was doing the calling, but that didn't matter while he ran, he ran, through bushes, creepers, tangles of creepers, a caterpillar dropped on him, he shuddered and brushed it off. There were cries behind him, shouts, screams, *ululations*, what a word that was, what a *sound* that was, what are the chances you would be ululated at two days in a row, no, not really, these were just screams, *just* screams, ha. That wrong turn cost him some valuable minutes, just keep running, what Debra said about exercise was right, what Debra said about pretty much everything was right, the exercise program begins now, today is the first day of the rest of my life he thought, as he ran, outside the Museum of Curiosities, it looked different in the dawn than in the moonlight. The path turned so he turned, around that abandoned house he had taken refuge in last night during the storm, until *it* was stormed, by stormtroopers, he thought as he kept running, his heart thrumping, thrumping, what a sound *that* was. The path turned again so he turned, came to a cliff, those cliffs, the beach below. He stopped, just a second, looked down below, a caterpillar dropped on him again, he shuddered and brushed it off and ran back around, outside and behind the values building, were they in there, was *he* in there, the covener and his coven, he found the path down the hill, down the hill. The woods were thicker here near the sanctuary, another caterpillar or was it two on him, the path turned so he turned, and then a squeal, a set of squeals, a herd of mini-pigs came squealing out of the greenery across his path but despite the shock of it all he kept running, ran through them, perhaps it was he who was squealing, he wondered whether he might be stepping in their droppings too late for that he thought as he twisted and turned through the path, twisted, then turned, then came out into a clearing, onto the remains of what had been, until recently, until very recently, a cookout.

On a stake inserted into the heart of the last ember was impaled a head, it was *a head*, for a moment it looked to him like *his head*—but no, of course no, it was the head of pig, *just* the head of pig, a little piglet, the coagulating blood still dripping slowly from the jagged edge of its neck down the stake. Its face, its terrible face, its squeal, its scream, capturing the moment of its death, the eternal moment of its death, its eyes, its terrible eyes, he looked straight into those ravaged eyes reflecting the growing glowing illumination of dawn—

They were covered in flies.

There were screams behind him, or perhaps it was just J. screaming as two or three caterpillars dropped on him and he ran straight through the embers, past the severed head, the screams behind him, more caterpillars dropping on him, dropping on him like flies, stumbling forward through the growth, the logs, the limbs, the broken limbs, from last night's storm, the horde stamping behind him, thinking about hate, about Hate, about hating Hate. J. forgot his wounds, his hunger and thirst, and became just fear, hopeless fear on flying feet, below him someone's legs were getting tired, they were his legs, and he was tired, he was so tired, could he just stop, he must not stop. Shaking off more caterpillars dropping like flies on him, more caterpillars all over him, he emerged from the edge of the woods onto a smoother path and the screaming right on his heels or maybe it was just him screaming and the dock, the dock wasn't much further, he was thinking, he was running, he was gasping, his heart pounding, the screaming, all over him they were all over him—when he stumbled, fell on his face, fell on the path—he was down, rolling over, bloodied, bruised, crouching with arm up to ward off, to prevent the flaying, to cry for mercy as the horde was to descend upon him—

"Hey there, you all right buddy?"

J., on the ground, was looking at a pair of white sneakers. His gaze slowly moved upward, into the bright sun just now rising over the water beyond, barely blocked by the silhouette of the uniformed figure standing in front of him. J. squinted at the man, squinted at the sun, suddenly understood the compass orientation of the island. *It's all backward*, he thought, *it's all backward*, having no idea what that meant. He squinted back up, just making out the man's white-topped naval cap with the little words, "The Ferry King," embroidered across them.

It was the ferry captain.

Behind him were several Japanese day-trippers, snapping photos of him on the ground.

There was silence except for the clicking of their cameras.

"What's going on here?" the captain asked, gently and kindly, perhaps with some humor. "Fun and games, it looks like? Nobody killed, I hope?"

J. shook his head, shook his head, shook his head, then rested it on his arms. He needed a bath, a haircut, a nose-wipe, and a good deal of—something.

They're just kids, he thought.

The tourists snapped more pictures.

The Last Word

You usually do get the last word, he says, so here you are. And where do you want me to start with the end, so to speak, I say? Your job I suppose, he says, is to connect the dots. So maybe I should start by generating a few dots.

First of all, the whole J. thing. I get it professionally, it's annoying to constantly have to explain your parents' supposed sense of humor. And I got it with the other book, for the same reason, he sold a few copies ridiculous as it was, he had a few minutes of fame, very *limited* fame, I remind him when he starts waxing about doing a follow-up, because the last thing anyone would be interested in would be more about my gargoyle of a family. But his parents (still kicking, in their eighties, God bless them) called and call him Jeffrey, I call him Jeffrey, even our boys have taken to calling him Jeffrey, in fact he introduces *himself* as Jeffrey. So I don't know what that is.

And as for the boys, the "monsters" as he calls them here, well the only time I have ever heard him use that word for them is in praise, such as "you were a monster on the soccer field today" or maybe "beware of the monster" when our oldest is destroying him at our basement foosball table. There's also his line about their being not three individual boys but a three-headed monster with six arms and six legs. That was definitely a good one the first twenty-five or thirty times I heard it. (For those taking notes that was banter, not bicker.) The reality is that he adores those little monsters, and they adore him, at least when he is not embarrassing them, which lately is almost always, but still.

They are fifteen, thirteen, and almost twelve, so of course that is normal. So calling them monsters is probably an attempt to be cool or something.

The uncool truth, the reality, is that for someone who allegedly was not keen to have children, and certainly not more than one, he has done pretty well as the father of three. And especially as the father of the third, who can be more than even the most dedicated child-desiring person could handle. That boy can find buttons you didn't even know you had and jab them all at once and repeatedly. But that photo from just last week, which one of their buddies in that parent-child league Jeffrey takes him to sent me, tells you everything you need to know. The boy was melting down, on the floor screaming right there on the lane, because the music at the alley that night was a little louder than usual. And there was Jeffrey down on the floor with him, holding him, squeezing him, his daddy protecting him until the world stopped assaulting him and he could get himself together. Took six or seven excruciating minutes, the league buddy told me. Jeffrey didn't even mention it when they came home.

So, no, I don't think he knows himself all that well. That's a little troubling because I trust him, I do trust him, in ways I don't like to admit. And believe me, I am not a trusting person, by nature or by nurture. (Read that other book if you want to learn more, although why you would want to is beyond me.) Actually I had to laugh when he has that crazy librarian saying all ominously, "Trust no one," because that is of course my line, as one far more skeptical of humankind than my much lesser half. I also had to laugh when he gave me, as part of his gift for my fiftieth-birthday a couple years back, that old French play, *The Misanthrope*. Why would I need to read this? I asked him, meaning I'm already the expert on that subject, but he took it the wrong way, thinking I was dismissing the gift. A few seconds of light banter turned into fifteen minutes of having to hash it out, figure out the meaning of it, talk about "the relationship." Happily it did work out at least that night, in fact I got a good laugh out of him later, when after a gobble-do-gee session of an intensity which, frankly, we hadn't had in a long while, I showed him that the subtitle to that play was even more apt than its title, "Or, the Cantankerous Lover." (For those taking notes, that lingo there is his infantile college pals' slang for oral sex.)

Maybe I should have left that last part out. God forbid my in-laws read this and the shock finally knocks one of them off.

Whatevs, as our fifteen-year old would say.

Or bam ba lam! as my annoying husband would say, who uses that annoying line from some obscure geezer rock song to mean everything from "Thank you" to "That's awesome" to "I find your ideas really interesting and would like to subscribe to your newsletter."

Sorry, I'm meandering. I like this last word thing. Which reminds me of the saying that women marry men hoping to change them, while men marry women hoping they never change. I don't know if that's entirely true but maybe it's a little bit true. I have had some success on small fronts. Years of inflicting decent cooking on him finally brought his pizza problem under control, for example. I also finally got him to do crossword puzzles with me once in a while. But far more challenging, and more important, has been my effort to make him a little more skeptical, a little less trusting, more misanthropic, why not. He may be in his mid-fifties already but maybe the old dog can still learn a new trick. It kills me how he lets people take advantage of him, for example. What can you expect, he says, from a man who prefers bruised fruits and vegetables at the supermarket because he yearns to give them a good home? I honestly thought that was only a line he gave me while we were dating but it turned out to be true: I swear the man lingers at the produce and deliberately chooses the worst of everything. It's pretty maddening. If you are going to let the fruit walk all over you, doc, I say to him, then how can you stand up for yourself against your conspecifics.

He says, what are conspecifics.

I say, other people.

He says he cannot tell if I am joking or not.

I say I am joking, but not really.

He says well that really clarifies.

I say Jeffrey, listen, why are you taking so many night calls at the hospital lately?

Because I can do the most good that way, be of most use, then.

No it's because your colleagues know you will let them get away with not taking their turns.

Even so, he says.

No not even so, I say. And why did you leave your private practice for the public hospital in the first place?

Because of the profit thing, the business end of it, I felt I could be more useful to more people working at the hospital, he says.

No it was because your partners wanted your share and filled your head with glorious ideas about public service medicine, I say.

He tells me I always see the dark side of things. I tell him that's because it's all dark, stealing that line from one of the geezer songs he idolizes, but he isn't amused. Well maybe he is, because he says well aren't you a little ray of pitch black, which is kind of funny because he also bought me a little desk plaque with that saying on it as part of my fiftieth-birthday gift. Maybe I'll get you your own copy of *The Misanthrope* for your sixtieth, I say. You are just way too easy on your conspecifics.

That whole "I'm a philosopher" thing, that was my idea, of course. People always want to talk to Jeffrey, he's got that sweet, innocent face that invites a conversation, but most of all he listens, he really listens, and once he opens that door people just barge right in. And what could be worse than people, especially people you don't know, telling you about all their problems, also involving people you don't know?

You should just tell people you're a philosopher, I say, and they'll leave you alone.

Why would I want them to leave me alone, he says.

Because that is the first in your ten-step program of becoming a misanthrope, I say.

And why would I want to do that, he says.

In order to please your wife who you love madly, I say. I thought all that was pretty funny, and the whole thing was meant as a joke, but then go figure, he took me seriously and actually started doing it. I thought well why not, let's see what happens. He stuck with it quite a while, even though he was never really comfortable with it. The lying thing bothered him, even though I told him it really wasn't lying if you were doing it as a joke, and he said great so now I have to really become a philosopher in order to decide if that is true.

Well if you really became a philosopher, then you wouldn't be lying, doc, now would you, I point out.

Once more, Debra, he concedes, you have outmaneuvered me in the domain of wit.

You mean outwitted you, I say.

He laughs but then stops.

Is this banter or bicker, he asks.

Banter, banter, I assure him.

But it wasn't just the lying that bothered him, it was the off-putting thing he didn't like, I don't like to put people off, he says. But I say great, then every bruised and broken person is going to unload their sad story on you, and he says Debra, you recall, I prefer the bruised and broken fruit and vegetables yadda-yadda. Great, I say, I bet you yearn to give these bruised and broken people a good home too but God knows we have enough bruised and broken people here already. He hesitates and says is *that* banter or bicker. I hesitate and say maybe neither, I'm sorry. It's funny or actually horrible how all things come back to, you know, the situation. The man already provides a good home to some pretty broken people so maybe I should go easier on him. But anyway it's all moot. I think he's done with the philosopher gig now, after whatever it was that happened at that so-called college he went to.

For those taking notes, I was all in favor of his going there. No, I didn't trust that Brenda woman for a second. I mean, bubbly sweaters and indiscriminate smiles? But first, honestly, and I know this may sound bad, I thought he might learn a useful lesson. Yes the philosopher thing backfired, that had happened a couple of times over the previous months, but for some reason Jeffrey hadn't yet drawn the general moral that the backfires were most dangerous of all. No good could ever come, I tell him, from people who become *more* interested in you when they think you are a philosopher, and I say that as someone who has spent a lot of my life in and around academementia.

Look your father was an exceptional case he starts to say.

It wasn't just my father, I interrupt.

Okay so your Ph.D. advisor was also an exceptional case, he starts to say.

You are kidding, right? I interrupt.

Okay the department chair was a jerk and one or two others but really there *were* others, decent people along the way, plenty of them, he says.

I say does that include the narcissists, the assholes, and the sexual harassers, and he says Debra I love you but you only see what you want to see and I say you can't steal my line about you, he says well I just did. Well look, I say, I can't quite predict what terrible thing will go wrong when people are drawn to you being a philosopher, but something will, so have at it, doc. Well aren't you a little ray of pitch black, he says, only this time it's a little less funny.

But here's the thing. That was a conversation we had once or twice (or maybe three or four times). To my credit this was not the conversation we had when he called me from the airport. There I was super supportive spouse, because contrary to popular belief I am not *entirely* dark myself. Yes I do think that most of our conspecifics are a calamity, but there *are* others, other decent people along the way, as my annoying husband puts it, and for better or for worse my annoying husband is among them. And yes he has been going through something the past couple of years. I actually think it is pretty normal—especially in light of the tragedy with his college friend which triggered it or certainly fueled it—and for those taking notes, I *am* a professional psychologist, but he points out that the fact that it is "normal" doesn't diminish its significance for him. I then point out that it should, because it means it is not a sign of deep-rooted pathology and it is something that will work itself out, and he points out that *that* fact doesn't diminish its significance either, and fine, I sort of admit that he is right. The technical term for what you are experiencing doc, I say, is a "funk," and while I need to do some more tests to be sure I think it will likely turn out to be an "existential funk." Basically, you are suffering from a textbook case of middle life what's it all about, Alfie. The jury is still out on whether your extra obsession with cadavers and flaying and dissection are cause for institutionalization.

I do have other hobbies you know, he says.

Bowling? Geezer rock music? Your collection of, what are they—

Narrenschiffen, he says, referring to his medieval miniatures that have some art-historical connection to cadavers, flaying, and dissection, and somehow also to geezer rock music.

I rest my case, I say, enjoying my last word in that conversation.

And the truth is that he *is* suffering from a funk—we sometimes call it "The Resistance" because it gets in his way everywhere, so now you know where *that* came from—and the reality is that I *am* worried, but I also know that if I reveal my concern that would only worry him further, because that would only get him worried about me too and because for whatever reason my annoying husband always trusts my judgments of things. You are the truth through and through the fool once told me when we were dating, and of course whenever I turn out to be right yet again about some social situation he likes to call me the Colonel of Truth.

And yet you resist when I suggest you see a therapist, I say.

I have *you*, he says, which annoys me on at least three different levels.

And you resist when I suggest you try some meds, I say.

But that is part of the problem, he says, as he has become hyper-concerned about the state of medical care today, in particular the role that the pharmaceutical and insurance companies play in the system. He is constantly reading studies, reports, late at night, online, to be honest he is developing an obsession with them too, almost conspiratorial in flavor. There's no doubt there is truth in there, individual truths maybe, but truths are just dots, I always say, and the real question is how you connect the dots.

My career is all about business now, he says, in his funk. Paperwork, insurance, billing, sales calls, bottom lines.

But most people's careers are about business, I say.

Yes but that is not why I went into this in the first place, he says.

Yes but that is ancient history now, I say, knowing what is coming. You know it is a surefire formula for misery, I say, wanting to change the past. Would and should do make you ill, doc, you know that.

I know, I know, but still, he says, entirely on cue, what if I had pursued my other interests, the art history, the gargoyles, literature, I don't know, maybe even writing.

You are not seriously what-iffing again, are you, I say, to *me*, the cursed woman of the what-if, the love of your life who, must I remind you, has categorically forbidden you from what-iffing?

Of course not, he says, and yet I cannot—

And-yetting, I interrupt, is just a form of what-iffing.

If only it weren't, he says, and we both sort of laugh, sort of.

And yet when the philosophy thing backfired, and this opportunity fell into his lap, super supportive spouse, to her credit, grabbed the phone from super cynical spouse and encouraged him to do it, for his sake. And he, to his credit, reproduced *that* conversation rather than our earlier ones where (as I think over them now) I do seem a little less than super supportive. And he reproduced that conversation more or less accurately, I should note, except that I didn't make that mistake about the podcast, I remembered perfectly correctly the guy who said you have maybe forty-five hundred hours in your life to do something worthwhile, because I remember everything. I think that was Jeffrey having a little fun with me there. But ha! he gave me the last word, so there.

And there was one other thing, that he left out. Yes, he was concerned that if he went to that so-called college he would have to extend his trip a couple of days. But the *reason* he was concerned was that he was worried about me and the boys, with my being alone with the boys those extra days, with me working full-time, on top of the full-time job that is our boys, on top of the full-time job that is our youngest boy all on his own. And he was worried about the boy. I told him that the older two could go out on their own, and that I could go out with that one, and that once we had worked through the inevitable costume meltdown, everything would be fine.

But we have an annual routine, he says.

He has to learn to be flexible, I say, sometimes.

He will be very upset with the change of routine, he says.

He has to learn to cope with upset, I say, my heart breaking, because we both know that he will never learn to cope with upset.

I'll come home, he says.

So that is when I did tell him that a little time apart is healthy for a relationship. I know that hurt him in the moment but I said it because otherwise he would not extend his trip, he would not take advantage of this really once-in-a-lifetime opportunity, he would once again put the boy or me or the boy *and* me before himself and for once my annoying husband needed to assert his own bam ba lam needs first. That little extra time apart just might be healthy for *him*.

So maybe I'm not all dark.

But maybe it's not *all* about me.

But then again, who can say what it *is* all about, Alfie. Maybe a little time apart *is* healthy for a relationship too, maybe? And no, I don't like sharing a bathroom with him, but I wouldn't like sharing a bathroom with *anyone*. And that line about not sharing a burial plot with him was entirely a joke but it too seems to have hurt his feelings. You would think that after more than two decades together I could just speak as I am, raw and unplugged, without censorship, without editing, but maybe I really should watch what I say to him. He also only hears what he wants to. Yours are impressions one cannot trust, I have said to him more than once. Especially since the funk. And he seems to have developed this notion that things are somehow less than perfect between us, that we're in some bad place. So with that notion he then interprets everything I say in the worst possible light. The same dots can be connected in different ways I tell him when, yet again, he has mistaken some moment of banter for bicker.

You are annoyed with me, he says.

No I am just concerned that you often think I am annoyed with you, I say.

Well then *now* you are annoyed with me, for thinking you are annoyed with me, he says.

I swear I am not, Jeffrey, I try to say as convincingly as I can, to convince him.

He says I have severe eyes when I am annoyed, though, and says my eyes are severe now. I realize I cannot see my own eyes to see their severity, and I do have to admit that sometimes, mostly accidentally, he manages to be right about this or that or the other. I start to wonder whether, maybe, by making him more skeptical of his conspecifics I have made him even skeptical of me. Or maybe, I also wonder, we *are* in some less than perfect place after all and *mine* are the impressions one cannot trust. I mean, I really *don't* want to share a bathroom or burial plot with him, now, do I?

Maybe even it is me who has made him feel like Alfie.

No, no, *no*, I say again, as convincingly as I can. What can I say to you so that you will accept what I say, I say.

What can you say, he says.

What can I say, I say.

All right, he says. You can say you love me.

"You love me," I say.

He hesitates. All right, he says, you can say "I love you."

You love me, I say, and I maybe see that I am breaking through.

And is there anything else, he says, you have to say.

You are asking for some sayings, I say.

Some sayings, he says, and there is a crack.

All right, so, I say, scratching my chin the way our middle son used to do when he was little, saying with his gentle lispy inability to say the "th" sound, "let me sink, let me sink." The optimist says this is the best possible world, I say. And the pessimist agrees.

Jeffrey reflects, nods. The masochist says beat me, he says. And the sadist says no.

My turn, let me sink. The sooner you fall behind, the more time you have to catch up, I say. So it's best to start falling behind immediately.

Was that a smile on his lips as he says, it's better to be profoundly wrong than superficially right, because then at least you are profound.

Oh, I say, and you are so good at being wrong!

He hesitates.

Banter, banter, I assure him quickly. He exhales, relaxes, my eyes are not severe. How am I? I say quickly, by every measure I am better off than ninety-nine percent of all people who have ever lived. And yet—

No and yets, he reminds me.

And yet, I say, my eyes not at all severe, worse off than—

the one percent, he says

I actually compare myself to, I finish.

He hesitates, he looks at me, he studies me.

One day, he says, we will be willing to give anything—

anything, I say

only to be able, he says

to come back, I say

to *this* day, he finishes.

We've been playing with this, these sayings, since the episode, obviously. It's great fun, and it sort of brings us back to our early days, before the years, before the children, before that child. We don't talk much about the episode itself now. He feels like he's told me everything, and besides, we have that issue, about what really happened. You know, I trust him with everything, my story, he is my witness, the one who helps me be sure that I am not the crazy one, and yet, sometimes he thinks we are bickering when we are bantering and bantering when we are bickering. Or at least when I think we are bantering and bickering. So you can maybe understand why I'm not absolutely one hundred percent sure about what happened at that so-called college. Maybe nothing happened there, I think sometimes, nothing serious anyway, a tempest in a teacup, they're just kids, their hearts are in the right place, maybe there was a misunderstanding. Unreasonable expectations, failure to meet them. Irony the fundamental tone of the universe, meaning is always in what's superfluous, yadda yadda. And my husband, he has that thing for the dramatic, the exaggeration, the embellishment. The mildly severe eye becomes a major crisis for the relationship. Just look at that other book, a pack of fantasies, I'm sure, as I would confirm if I could ever bring myself to read it.

But then on the other hand he does sometimes get it right, underneath, or buried inside, the fiction.

So what really happened?

In the end it's probably better not to look at it all too closely.

What, anyway, could be gained by doing so? If it did happen as he says it did, it was a calamity; and also if it didn't. That's why I haven't looked at that student newspaper website to see what they say happened. And God forbid he were to catch me checking on his story. My poor husband can be so damn sensitive to questions about interpretation and misinterpretation, especially living with our youngest, who is so misconnected to the world that when you say good morning to him he can experience *that* as an assault. If Jeffrey caught me checking the severe eyes would be his. No, not severe; deflated, destroyed. I couldn't do that to him.

And more importantly he has been feeling so much better since the episode that the last thing I want to do is poke that sleeping dog. He was cloudy then, he says, but now has clarity. Adrift for a while, but now he feels anchored again.

What is different, I ask.

Was and will do make you ill, he says, but he has found his way back to factuality, to here, to now, to us, and all that.

That sounds delightful, I say, but is "factuality" a word, in actuality?

He ignores me by again quoting one of the various philosophy books he has been reading ever since he was a philosopher and in a funk. The "real," he starts to explain, is a synthesis of perception and conception. I personally think that is absurd because the "real" is whatever is out there no matter what we think of it, but I merely say, so? So? he echoes as if it's the most obvious thing, if too much percept is our Scylla, then too much concept is our Charybdis. Well that really clarifies, I say. Don't you see, he sighs, don't you see, it makes you ill because the infinite both is and is not here, the eternal both is and is not now, and all humanity is and is not us. I am tempted to say bam ba lam I would like to subscribe to your newsletter, but instead I have to admit, grudgingly, that I sort of get it, that there is some kernel of truth in there. I sort of get that when it comes to matters of meaning, as far as anything can really matter to you, the real *is* what you take it to be. But then it's not only that you can connect the same dots in different ways but that in doing so you may partly be constructing the very dots in the first place. One day, we say, we will be willing to give *anything* to be able to come back to this day. This day, today, is and is not eternity. And so I don't push the question of what really happened at that so-called college.

It's all true, he says, all of it, except for the parts that aren't.

And the parts that aren't, he says, are most true of all.

And with that I guess I give *him* the last word.

Oh wait.